Please return/renew this item by the last date shown

**Herefordshire
Libraries**

**Herefordshire
Council**

Works by Adrian McKinty published by Serpent's Tail

The Dead Trilogy
Dead I Well May Be
The Dead Yard
The Bloomsday Dead

The Sean Duffy thrillers
The Cold Cold Ground
I Hear the Sirens in the Street
In the Morning I'll Be Gone
Gun Street Girl
Rain Dogs
Police at the Station and They Don't Look Friendly

Hidden River
Fifty Grand
Falling Glass
The Sun is God

ADRIAN McKINTY

POLICE AT THE STATION AND THEY DON'T LOOK FRIENDLY

Words and music by Thomas Waits and Kathleen Brennan
© Copyright Jalma Music administered by Native Tongue Music Publishing Pty Ltd
All print rights for Australia and New Zealand administered by
Hal Leonard Australia Pty Ltd ABN 13 085 333 713
www.halleonard.com.au
Used By Permission. All Rights Reserved. Unauthorised Reproduction is Illegal.

First published in Great Britain in 2017 by Serpent's Tail,
an imprint of Profile Books Ltd
3 Holford Yard
Bevin Way
London
WC1X 9HD
www.serpentstail.com

1 3 5 7 9 10 8 6 4 2

Designed and typeset by Crow Books

Printed and bound by CPI Group (UK) Ltd, Croydon, CR0 4YY

A CIP record for this book can
be obtained from the British Library

ISBN 978 1 78125 693 0
eISBN 978 1 78283 279 9

Police at the station and they don't look friendly,
Police at the station and they don't look friendly to me . . .
Tom Waits, "Cold Water", 1992

It only takes two facing mirrors to construct a labyrinth.
Jorge Luis Borges, *Seven Nights*, 1977

PROLOGUE: YOU CAN'T TRUST A SPECIAL LIKE THE OLD-TIME COPPERS

Blue dark, red dark, yellow dark.

Snow glinting in the hollows. The Great Bear and the Pole Star visible between zoetroping tree limbs.

The wood is an ancient one, a relic of the vast Holocene forest that once covered all of Ireland but which now has almost completely gone. Huge oaks half a millennium old; tangled, many-limbed hawthorns; red-barked horse chestnuts.

"I don't like it," the man behind the man with the gun says.

"Just put up with it, my feet are getting wet too," the man with the gun replies.

"It's not just that. It's these bloody trees. I can hardly see anything. I don't like it. It's spooky, so it is."

"Ach, ya great girl ya, pull yourself together."

But it is indeed spooky out here, in the hulking shadows of these venerable oaks, four hours after midnight, in the middle of nowhere, while Ireland sleeps, while Ireland dreams . . .

The little rise is a deceptively steep incline that takes my breath away and I can see that I am going to need my new inhaler if it keeps up. The inhaler, of course, is back in the glove compartment of the car because I haven't yet acquired the habit of taking it with me everywhere. Not that it will make any difference in a few minutes anyway. A bullet in the head will fix an incipient asthma attack every time.

"Hurry up there," the man with the gun growls and for emphasis pokes the ugly snub nose of the revolver hard into my back.

I say nothing and continue to trudge at the same pace through the nettle banks and ferns and over huge, lichen-covered yew roots.

We walk in silence for the next few minutes. Victim. Gunman. Gunman's assistants. It is a cliché. This exact scene has played out at least a thousand times since 1968 all over rural Ulster. I myself have been the responding officer on half a dozen bodies found face down in a sheugh, buried in a shallow grave or dumped in a slurry pit on the high bog. The victims always show ligature marks on the wrists where they have been cuffed or tied and the bullet is always a headshot behind the left or right ear usually from less than a metre away and almost always from above.

Trudge, *trudge*, *trudge* we go up the hill, following a narrow forest trail.

If I was so inclined I could believe in the inherent malevolence of this place: moonlight distorting the winter branches into scarecrows, the smell of rotting bog timber, and just beyond the path, in the leaf litter on the forest floor, those high-pitched unsettling sounds that must be the life-and-death skirmishes of small nocturnal animals. But the pathetic fallacy has never been my cup of tea and I'm no romantic either. Neither God, nor nature, nor St Michael the Archangel, the patron saint of policemen, is coming to save me. *I* have to save me. These men are going to kill me unless *I* can talk or fight my way out of it.

A fire-break in the forest.

Sky again.

Is the blue a little lighter in the east? Maybe it's later than I thought. The interrogation didn't seem to go on too long but you lose track of time when you're tied to a chair with a hood on your head. Could it be five in the morning? Five thirty? They've taken my watch so I can't know for sure but wasps and bluebottles are beginning to stir and if you listen you can hear the first hints of the morning chorus: blackbirds, robins, wood pigeon. Too early in the year for cuckoos, of course.

Who is going to teach Emma about the birds and their calls when they shoot me? Will Beth still drive out to Donegal so Emma can spend time with her grandparents? Probably not. Probably Beth will move to England after this.

Maybe that would be for the best anyway.

There's no future in this country.

The future belongs to the men behind me with the guns. They're welcome to it. Over these last fifteen years I've done my best to fight entropy and carve out a little local order in a sea of chaos. I have failed. And now I'm going to pay the price of that failure.

"Come on, Duffy, no slacking now," the man with the gun says.

We cross the fire-break and enter the wood again.

Just ahead of us on the trail a large old crow flaps from a hawthorn branch and alerts all the other crows that we are blundering towards them.

Caw, caw, caw!

Always liked crows. They're smart. As smart as the cleverest dog breeds. Crows can recall human faces for decades. They know the good humans and the bad humans. When these thugs forget what they've done to me this morning the crows will remember.

Comforting that. My father taught me the calls and the collective nouns of birds before I even knew my numbers. *Murder of crows, unkindness of ravens, kit of wood pigeon, quarrel of—*

"Don't dilly-dally, get a move on there, Duffy! I see what you're about! Keep bloody walking," the man with the gun says.

"It's the slope," I tell him and look back into his balaclava-covered face.

"Don't turn your head, keep walking," he says and pokes me

in the back with the revolver again. If my hands weren't cuffed I could use one of those pokes to disarm him the way that Jock army sergeant taught us in self-defence class back in 1980. When you feel the gun in your back you suddenly twist your whole body perpendicular to the gunman, presenting only air as your hands whip around and grab his weapon hand. After that it's up to you – break the wrist and grab the gun or kick him in the nuts and grab the gun. The Jock sergeant said that you've got about a 75 per cent chance of successfully disarming your opponent if you're fast enough. Lightning turn, speedy grab, no hesitation. We all knew that the sergeant had pulled those statistics right out of his arse but even if it was only one chance in ten it was better than being shot like a dog.

Moot point this morning, though. My hands are behind my back in police handcuffs. Even if I do spin round fast enough I can't grab the gun and if I suddenly make a break for it I am sure to fall over or get shot in the back.

No, my best chance will be if I can talk to them, try to persuade them; or if that doesn't work (and it almost certainly won't) then I'll have to try something when they uncuff me and give me the shovel to dig my own grave. I will certainly be going into a grave. If they just wanted to kill a copper, they would have shot me at the safe house and dumped my body on a B road and called the BBC. But not me, me they have been told to *disappear*. Hence this walk in the woods, hence the man behind the man with the gun carrying a shovel. The question is why? Why does Duffy have to disappear when killing a peeler would be a perfect morale boost for the cause at this time?

There can only be one reason why. Because if my body actually shows up it'll bring heat on Harry Selden and Harry Selden, despite his professions of innocence, does not want heat.

The gradient increases and I try to calm my breathing.

Easy does it now, Sean, easy does it.

I walk around a huge fallen oak lying there like a dead god.

The earth around the oak is soft and I slip on a big patch of lichen and nearly go down.

"Cut that out!" the man with the gun growls as if I've done it on purpose.

I right myself somehow and keep walking.

Don't dilly-dally, he said earlier.

You don't hear that expression much any more. He must be an older man. Older than he sounds. I might be able to talk to a man like that . . .

Out of nowhere a song comes back to me, played 4/4 time by my grandfather on the concertina:

My old man said "Foller the van, and don't dilly dally on the way".

Off went the van wiv me 'ome packed in it, I followed on wiv me old cock linnet.

But I dillied and dallied. Dallied and dillied,

Now you can't trust a special like the old-time coppers,

When you're lost and broke and on your uppers . . .

The concertina playing is note perfect but the singing . . . my grandfather, who was from a very well-to-do street in Foxrock, Dublin, can't do a Cockney accent to save his life.

Isn't that strange, though? The whole song, lurking there in my memory these twenty-five years.

Oh yes, concertinas look fiendishly complicated, Sean, but they're easy when you get the hang of them.

Really?

Sure. Have a go, let me show you how to—

"Jesus, will you hurry up, you peeler scum!" the man with the gun says. "You think you have nothing to lose? We don't have to make this quick, you know. We don't have to be easy on you."

"This is you going easy?"

"We've let you keep your bollocks, haven't we?"

"I'm going as fast as I can. You try walking through this lot with your hands cuffed behind your back. Maybe if you undid these handcuffs, which you've put on far too tight anyway."

"Shut up! No one told you to speak. Shut up and keep bloody moving."

"OK. OK."

Trudge, trudge, trudge up the hill.

The slope increases again and the forest is thinning out. At the edge of it I can see sheep fields and hills and perhaps to the north that dark smudge is the Atlantic Ocean. We are only a forty-five minute drive from Belfast, but we are in another world completely, far from planes and machines, far from the visible face of the war. Another Ireland, another age. And yes, the stars are definitely less clear now, the constellations fading into the eggshell sky. Dawn is coming, but dawn won't save me. I'll be dead before sun-up if they are even halfway competent, which I think they are.

"What is the matter with them?" the man with the gun mutters to himself. "Hurry up you two!" he yells to the others.

I've been told not to look back, but this confirms what I've suspected. Of the five men who lifted me, one is waiting back at the car, one is waiting at the bottom of the trail to be a look-out and the other three are going to do the deed itself.

"All right, no one told you to stop, keep going, Duffy!" the man with the gun says.

I shake my head. "I need to catch my breath. I'm asthmatic," I reply. "I'm having trouble breathing."

"There's nothing wrong with you!"

"I'm asthmatic. They diagnosed it at my physical."

"What physical?"

"My police physical. I thought it was just too much smoking but the doctor said I had developed asthma. I've got an inhaler."

"Rubbish!"

"It's true."

"Did you bring your inhaler?"

"Nope. It's back in the glove compartment of my car."

"What's going on? Are we going to top him here?" one of the two others asks, catching us up. The one complaining about the spooky trees. The one with the shovel.

"He claims he's got asthma. He says he can't breathe," the man with the gun says.

"Aye, cold morning like that will give it to you. Our Jack has asthma," this second man says. Younger than the man with the gun, he's wearing a denim jacket, tight bleached jeans and white sneakers. The shovel is an old model: heavy wooden handle, cast-iron blade, low centre of gravity . . .

"I don't believe in asthma. Asthma's a modern invention. Fresh air is all you need," the man with the gun says.

"Well, you can talk to our Jack's mum, she's been to the best doctors on the Waterside, so she has."

The third man reaches us. He's smaller than the others. He's wearing a brown balaclava and a flying jacket.

No, not *he*. It's a woman. She didn't speak during the car ride but if I'd been smarter I would have twigged that that smell in the back was her perfume. Thought it was the car's air freshener. She also is carrying a gun. An old .45. Look at that gun. US Army issue. 1930's model ACP. That's been in somebody's shoebox since the GIs were here in WW2. There wouldn't be any suffering with a weapon like that. Wouldn't even hear the shot. An instantaneous obliteration of consciousness. Wouldn't feel anything. Sentience into darkness just like that. And then, if Father McGuigan is correct, an imperceptible passage of time followed by the resurrection of the body at the End of Days . . .

"Is this it? Is this the spot?" she asks.

"No, we've a wee bit to go yet," the man with the revolver says.

"Can we just do it here, we're miles from everybody," shovel man wonders.

"We do it where we're told to do it," the leader insists. "It's not far now, anyway. Here, let me show you."

He unfolds a home-made map on thick, coarse paper. It's like no cartography I have ever seen, filled with esoteric symbols and pictograms and mysterious crisscrossing paths and lines. The guy's an eccentric who makes his own maps. In other circumstances entirely we'd probably get on like a house on fire.

"What is this? Some new thing from the Ordnance Survey?" the woman asks.

"No! God no. 'Ordnance Survey', she says."

"What is it?"

"Each one of us should make a surveyor's map of his lost fields and meadows. Our own map. With our own scale and legend," the man with the gun says.

"What do you mean 'our lost fields'?" the woman says irritably.

"He's quoting Gaston Bachelard," I say.

"Who asked you? Shut up!" the man with the gun snaps.

"Gaston who?" the man with the shovel wonders.

"Look him up. There's more to life than the pub, the bookies and the dole office, you know. Asthma my arse! There is no asthma. Have you noticed that none of us have fallen? Have you noticed how quickly our feet have become accustomed to the ground?" the man with the gun says.

"Not really," the woman replies.

"For the last half hour our eyes have been secreting rhodopsin. We're adapting to the dark. That's why you have to get outside, away from artificial illumination. Good for the eyes, good for the soul."

"Rhodopsin?" the woman asks.

"It's a protein receptor in the retina. It's the chemical that rods use to absorb photons and perceive light. The key to night vision."

"What on earth are you talking about, Tommy?" the woman says.

"No names!"

"Ach what does it matter if we use our names? Sure *he*'s going to be dead soon, anyway," the man with the shovel says.

"Doesn't matter if he's going to be dead or not. It's the protocol! No names. Did youse *ever* listen during the briefings? Bloody kids!" *Tommy* mutters and folds away his map in a huff.

"Is it much further?" the woman asks.

"Come on, let's get moving," Tommy shouts, pointing the gun at me again.

Trudge, trudge, trudge up the hill, but it must be said that I have learned much in this little interaction. The man with the gun is about forty-five or fifty. A school biology teacher? All that stuff about protein receptors . . . No, he probably read all that in *New Scientist* magazine and remembered it. Not biology. Doesn't seem like the type who was smart enough to get a pure science degree. Geography, maybe. Bit of a hippy, probably a lefty radical, and that was definitely a Derry accent. We almost certainly went to the same rallies in the early 70s. Definitely a Catholic too, which would mean he's probably a teacher at St Columb's, St Joseph's or St Malachy's. That's a lot to work with. And he's the leader, a couple of decades older than the other two. If I can turn him the rest will snap into line.

A big if.

"Rhodopsin my foot. I fell," shovel man says, passing the woman the water bottle. "Twice. And it's going to be worse going downhill. Mark my words. We'll all be going arse over tit. You'll see."

The woods are thinning out a bit now and in the far west I can see headlights on a road. Ten miles away, though and going in the other direction. No help from there.

A gust of clear, elemental wind blows down from the hilltop. I'm only wearing jeans and a T-shirt and my DMs. At least it's my lucky Che Guevara T-shirt, hand-printed and signed by Jim Fitzpatrick himself. If a dog walker or random hiker finds my body a few years hence and the T-shirt hasn't decayed maybe they'll be able to identify me from that.

"Careful on this bit!" Tommy says. "It's mucky as anything. There's a bog hole over there. Dead ewe in it. But once we're through that, we're there."

We wade through a slew of black tree roots and damp earth and finally arrive at a dell in the wood that must be the designated execution spot.

It's a good place to kill someone. The ring of trees will muffle the gun shots and the overhanging branches will protect the killers from potential spying eyes in helicopters and satellites.

"We're here," Tommy says, looking at his map again.

"There must have been a better way to come than this," shovel man says, exhausted. "Look at my trainers. These were brand new gutties! Nikes. They are soaked through to the socks."

"That's all you can say? Look at my gutties! Complain, complain, complain. Do you have no sense of decorum? This is a serious business. Do you realise we're taking a man's life this morning?" Tommy says.

"I realise it. But why we have to do it in the middle of nowhere halfway up a bloody mountain I have no idea."

"And here's me thinking you'd appreciate the gravity of the task, or even a wee bit of nature. Do you even know what these are?" Tommy asks, pointing at the branches overhead.

"Trees?"

"*Elm* trees! For all we know maybe the last elm trees in Ireland."

"Elm trees my arse."

"Aye, as if you know trees. You're from West Belfast," Tommy snarls.

"There are trees in Belfast. Trees all over the shop! You don't have to live in a forest to know what a bloody tree is. You know who lives in the woods? Escaped mental patients. Place is full of them. And cultists. Ever see *The Wicker Man*? And big cats. Panthers. *The Sunday World* has a photograph of—"

"Gentlemen, please," the woman says, reaching us. "Are we finally here, or what?"

"We're here," Tommy mutters.

"Well let's get this over with then," she says.

"Uncuff him and give him the spade," Tommy says.

Shovel man uncuffs me and leaves the shovel on the ground next to me. All three of them stand way back to give me room.

"You know what to do, Duffy," Tommy says.

"You're making a big mistake," I say to him, looking into his brown eyes behind the balaclava. "You don't realise what you're doing. You're being used. You're—"

Tommy points the revolver at my crotch.

"I'll shoot you in the bollocks if you say one more word. I'll make you dig with no nuts. Now, shut up and get to work."

I rub my wrists for a moment, pick up the shovel and start to dig. The ground is damp and soft and forgiving. It won't take me ten minutes to dig a shallow grave through this stuff.

Everyone is staying well out of shovel-swinging range. They may be new at this, but they're not stupid.

"I'll be glad when this is over," the woman whispers to the younger man. "I'm dying for a cup a tea."

"And I could do with a ciggie. Can't believe I left them back at the farm," he replies.

"Tea and cigarettes is all they can think about when we're taking a man's life," Tommy growls to himself.

"It's easy for you, you don't smoke. I . . ."

I turn down the volume so they're nothing more than back-ground noise.

I think of Beth and Emma as I dig through a surprising line of chalk in all this peat. *Chalk.*

Emma's smile, Beth's green eyes.

Emma's laugh.

Let that be the last thing in my consciousness. Not the babel of these misguided fools.

Shovel.

Earth.

Shovel.

Always knew that death was a strong possibility in my line of work, but it was absurd that that banal case of the dead drug dealer in Carrickfergus could have led to this. As standard a homicide as you're ever likely to see in Ulster. Ridiculous.

Earth.

Shovel.

Earth.

Shovel.

Gasping for . . .

Having trouble breathing again.

Gasping for—

Gasping for—

They think I'm faking it.

I have taxed their patience.

Someone pushes me and I go down.

Spreadeagled on my back in the black peat.

"Let's just top him now," a voice says from a thousand miles away.

"Yeah, all right."

Above me tree-tops, crows, sky.

And the yellow dark, the red dark, and the deep blue dark . . .

1: NO HAY BANDA

County Donegal is certainly not the wettest place on planet
Earth; 130 inches of rain a year in Donegal may be a typical
average high, but that's nothing compared to, say, Mawsynram
in India, where over 400 inches of rain can fall in a calendar
year. Crucially, however, that rain comes during the monsoon
and the monsoon only lasts for about ten weeks. The rest of
the year in Mawsynram is probably rather pleasant. One can
imagine walking in the foothills of the Himalayas or perhaps
taking a guided excursion to the tea plantations of Barduar.
Donegal may not have the sheer amount of precipitation of
Mawsynram but it makes up for this in the dogged persistence
of its rain. Rain has been measured in some parts of Donegal
on 300 days out of the year and if you add in the days of mist,
mizzle and snow you could be looking at a fortnight in which
some form of moisture does not fall to earth.

It is somewhat of a paradox then that until the arrival of cheap
packet flights to Spain, Donegal was the preferred holiday des-
tination for many people in Northern Ireland. All my childhood
holidays were taken in Donegal at a succession of bleak cara-
van sites on windswept, cold, rainy beaches. Scores of parents
wrapped in thick woollen jumpers and sou'westers could be
seen up and down these beaches driving their small, shivering
children into the Atlantic Ocean with the injunction that they
could not come out until they had enjoyed themselves.

My memories of Donegal had never been particularly good ones and when my father took early retirement and my parents moved to a cottage near Glencolumbkille I was a reluctant visitor.

Things had changed, of course, with the birth of Emma. My folks demanded to see their granddaughter and Beth and I had driven out there for Christmas and now here we were again in the early spring. Glencolumbkille is in the Gaeltacht, with almost everyone in these parts speaking the quaint Donegal version of Irish. It is a little whitewashed place straight out of *The Quiet Man* with a spirit grocer, a post office, a pub, a chapel, a golf course, a small hotel, a beach and a cliff-path. A pleasant enough spot if you didn't mind rain or boredom or the hordes of embedded high-school students from Dublin practising their Irish on you. One of these kids stopped me when I was out getting the milk. "Excuse me, sir. *An gabh tu pios caca?*"

"No I would not like any cake, thank you."

He tried again, this time apparently asking for the way to the bandstand.

I explained in slow, patient Irish that there was neither a bandstand nor a band in Glencolumbkille.

He cocked his head to one side, puzzled.

"There is no bandstand. There is no band. *No hay banda, il n'est pas une orchestra.*"

"Oh, I see," he said in English. "No I was looking for the way to the beach hut, we're supposed to meet at the beach hut."

"It's just over there *on the beach*. And the word you're looking for is *bothán trá.*"

"Thanks very much, pops," he said and sauntered off.

"Pops, indeed," I muttered as I bought the milk and a local paper and I was still muttering as I walked back to the house where Mum and Beth were talking about books.

My mother, Mary, had taken immediately to Beth, despite her being a Protestant, monolingual, well off, younger and, worst of all, not a fan of Dolly Parton.

"Don't you even like 'Little Sparrow'?" she had asked on hearing about this calamity.

"I'm so sorry, Mrs Duffy, it's just not my cup of tea. But I'll listen again if you want me to," Beth had said conciliatingly.

This morning they were talking about Beth's master's thesis which she was trying to do on Philip K. Dick, something the stuffy English department at Queens were none too happy about. My mother's sympathies lay with Queens, as, secretly, did mine.

"But Mr Dick, apparently, is only just deceased. You can't tell if a writer's any good or not until they're dead a generation, at least," Mum was saying.

Beth looked at me for support but there was no way I was stepping into that minefield.

"Milk," I said, putting the carton on the kitchen table. "And I've brought Dad his paper," I added quickly, before nimbly exiting and leaving them to it.

My father also had taken to Beth and he discovered that he enjoyed the company of his daughter-in-law and granddaughter so much that while we were here he even, temporarily, lost all interest in his beloved golf and bird-watching. At night he would talk to us in low tones about Emma's prodigious achievements in ambulation, speech and the manipulation of wooden blocks.

"Talking at six months! And almost walking. You can see it. She wants to walk. Standing there, thinking about it. She said 'Grand-pa'! I heard her. That girl is a genius. I'm serious, Sean. You should start speaking to her in French and Irish. She'll be fluent by the time she's one. And you should have seen her make that Lego tower. Incredible . . ."

My parents' cottage faced the ocean and at the far end of the house there was a little soundproof library with a big double-glazed plate-glass window that looked west. Dad's record player was over twenty years old and his speakers were shite, but his collection was eclectic and pretty good. Since moving to Donegal he had discovered the works of the English composer Arnold Bax, who had spent much of the 1920s in Glencolumbkille.

I walked down to the library, found a comfy chair to look through the local newspaper and put on Bax's really quite charming "November Woods". Dad came in just after the strange, muted climax which was so reminiscent of the instrumental music of the early Michael Powell films.

"Hello, Sean, am I bothering you?"

"No, Da, not at all. Just listening to one of your records. Arnold Bax isn't bad, is he?"

"No, you're right there. He's wonderful. There's a lightness of touch but it's not insubstantial or frivolous. His heyday was the same time as that of Bix Beiderbecke. It's a pity they couldn't of played together. Bax and Bix. You know?"

"Yes, Dad," I said, stifling a groan.

He sat down in the easy chair next to me. He was sixty-five now, but with a full head of white hair and a ruddy sun-tanned face from all the birding and golfing, he looked healthy and good. He could have passed for an ageing French *flaneur* if he hadn't been dressed in brown slacks, brown sandals (with white socks) and a "Christmas" jumper with reindeers on it.

He handed me the *Irish Times* crossword and a thesaurus. I gave him the thesaurus back. "That's cheating," I said. "What clue is bothering you?"

"Nine down."

"Nine down: 'Melons once rotten will drop off branches.' It's *somnolence*, Dad. It's an anagram of *melons once*."

"Oh, I see. This is the world's worst thesaurus anyway. Not only is it terrible, it's terrible," he said and began to chuckle with such suppressed mirth that I thought he was going to do himself a mischief.

"Are you still on for tomorrow?" he asked. "I've been sensing that you don't want to do it, son."

My father's senses were completely correct. I didn't want to do it. Tomorrow we were driving to Lough Derg, about fifteen minutes inland from here, where we were going to get the boat over to Station Island for the St Patrick's Purgatory pilgrimage. You could do the pilgrimage twice a year: in the summer (which is when nearly everyone did it) or during Lent. The whole thing had got started 1,500 years earlier when, to encourage St Patrick with his mission among the Godless Irish, Jesus Christ had come down from heaven and shown St Patrick a cave on Station Island that led all the way down to Purgatory. Ever since then it had been an important place of pilgrimage for devout Catholics from all over Europe. My father had never been a devout Catholic but his interest in Lough Derg had been kindled by Seamus Heaney's new book-length poem "Station Island" about his own pilgrimage to Lough Derg. Heaney's poem and his slew of amiable interviews all over Irish TV and radio had made the place sound spiritually and philosophically fascinating and in a moment of weakness I had agreed to my father's request to accompany him; but now, of course, that we were on the eve of our journey I was not bloody keen at all. The idea of spending three days fasting and praying with my dad while walking barefoot around a damp, miserable island with a bunch of God-bothering weirdos didn't sound like my idea of fun.

"Oh, Sean, I'm glad you're still enthusiastic. It'll be good for all of us. Beth, Mary and Emma will get some quality time together and you and I will get closer. Maybe even closer to God, too."

"I thought you didn't believe in God. That's what you told Father Cleary."

"Well, Sean, when you get to my age, you think to yourself that there's more things in Heaven and Earth . . . you know?"

I didn't know if I believed in God either but I believed in St Michael the patron saint of policemen and I owed my thanks to

The Blessed Virgin, who, I reckoned, had helped change Beth's mind about the abortion in Liverpool nearly a year ago.

"Wouldn't you rather do the pilgrimage in the summer like normal people?" I asked.

"Nope. The Pope says that if you do a pilgrimage to one of the traditional sites during Lent it'll be particularly blessed, so it will."

"Hark onto Alfred Duffy quoting the Pope. Alfred Duffy who forced Dr McGuinness to teach us about Darwin. What's happened to you, Da? Did you get hit in the head with a golf ball or something?"

He grinned and leaned back in the chair, his watery blue eyes twinkling. "Oh, I just remembered what I wanted to ask you. You're on for the quiz tonight? We've never won yet, but with you on our team I think we have a good chance of beating the GAA."

"Will it be in English? If Beth wants to come?"

Dad smiled at the mention of Beth's name. "Ah, you got a good one there. You know it doesn't bother us that she's a, you know . . ."

"Red-head?"

"Protestant."

"Is she a Prod? I hadn't noticed. Well that explains everything."

"All you have to do now is marry her and your mother will be in clover."

"A wedding? Come on, Da. All our lot down one side of the church, them lot down the other?" I said, not mentioning the fact that Beth had told me never to even think about proposing to her. "And Beth's father isn't exactly a fan of mine," I added.

"What does he do again?"

"Builds houses."

"He works with his hands. I like that."

"Like Gwendolyn Fairfax I doubt very much if he's ever seen a spade. He got the firm from his father. All he seems to do is sit in his office and think up the street names for all his new developments."

"What does he name them?"

"Mostly after obscure members of the royal family. Some Bible stuff. I only met the man twice and if I hadn't been armed with my Glock I think he would have tried to beat me to death with one of his golf clubs."

"Ah, golfer is he? He can't be all bad. What's his handicap?"

"Handicap? Well, he's got an eighteenth-century mind-set, he's stinking rich and for recreation he golfs at Down Royal or sails about on his bloody great yacht. Is that handicap enough?"

"Yes, you've said she comes from money. Down Royal though. I'd love to play that course. You couldn't possibly ask if I—"

"No, I couldn't! I've told you, he's not my biggest fan."

"Maybe if you made what they used to call 'an honest woman' of his daughter he wouldn't be so hostile."

"Dad, trust me, a wedding is not in the cards."

"Well, I'm not going to try to force you. Every time I've tried to force you to do anything it hasn't worked. Backfired in me face, so it has. I still regret sending you off to that bird-watching camp on Tory Island. You cried and cried and I don't think you ever picked up a birding book again after that."

"Damn right. To this day I can't tell the difference between a woodcock and a bog snipe," I said and my father, who was easily pleased, erupted into gales of laughter (for, of course, as I'm sure you know, a woodcock and a bog snipe are the same thing).

Dinner that night was a high-spirited affair. One of Dad's neighbours had caught a massive sea bass and mum had cooked it in a white wine sauce with scallops and potatoes while Beth and I took Emma down the beach to throw stones at the breakers.

We sat in the dining room under the portraits of JFK and the Derby-winning horse Shergar (both assassinated in their prime) while a turf fire burned in the range and rain lashed the windows.

Beth, Emma and Mum stayed at home while Dad and I trudged to The Lost Fisherman for the village's big event of the week if you didn't count mass on Sunday (and fewer and fewer people did, with each fresh week bringing a fresh church scandal). Dad introduced me to all his golfing cronies and told them that with me on the team we were sure to crush those arrogant bastards from the GAA.

In the event the GAA performed poorly and by the final general knowledge round it was between the golf club and the bowling club for the prize pool of fifty quid. Marty O'Reilly said that there would be a tie-break question.

"This is the question and I want you to be very precise with your answer. No shouting out from any of the other teams. All right, here goes. What were the very first words spoken from the Apollo 11 astronauts on the surface of the moon? Everybody get that? Good. As usual, write your answers on the card and bring them up. I'll give you two minutes to think about it. Stop that! No whispering from any of the other teams!"

"The very first words from the moon?" Davy Smith said in a panic but I knew there was no need to worry because my dad was grinning to himself.

"Never fret, Alfred knows," I said.

"Do you know right enough, Alfred?" Big Paul McBride asked.

"Look over there at them bowling boys. They think they know the answer but they don't!" Dad said, almost rubbing his hands with glee.

"What's that supposed to mean, Da?"

"A lot of people think the first words spoken on the surface of the moon are 'That's one small step for man – that's one giant leap for mankind.' But it's not. It's not even 'That's one small step for *a* man', which Armstrong claims he says. That's what Armstrong said when he first stepped off the bottom rung of the ladder of the lunar lander, but him and Aldrin had been talking in there for an hour by then."

"What is it then?" Jeanie Coulhouln asked, on the edge of her seat.

"I'll tell you what else it's not, it's not 'Houston, the Eagle has landed', either. Everyone thinks it's that, but it's not that," Dad insisted.

"OK that's what it's not. What's the right answer?" Jeanie asked.

"Well," my father began, smiling at us beatifically like the Venerable Bede. "Not many people know this, but as the lunar lander, the Lem, as it was called, was touching down on the moon they had a little light to let them know when they'd actually touched down. It was the contact light and as soon as they touched down on the surface Buzz Aldrin had to tell Armstrong that the contact light was on so he could turn off the engines. So they touch down and the light comes on and Aldrin says 'Contact light', ergo the very first words spoken on the moon were 'Contact light'."

"Are you sure now, Alfred?" Big Paul said, poised with his pen. "This'll be the first time we've ever won outright."

"I'm sure," Dad insisted.

We wrote our answer on the card. The bowling club wrote down their answer and we both handed the cards up to Marty.

Marty grabbed the microphone and dramatically shook his pinched, aged face from side to side. "Ladies and gentlemen, you are not going to believe it! Both teams got the wrong answer! Both teams got it wrong so this week there's no clear winner and we're going to divide the pot. The bowlers wrote 'That's one small step for man' and the golf club lost their heads completely and wrote 'Contact light', but the right answer, is, of course: 'Houston, the Eagle has landed'!"

When we got home the rain had stopped, so Beth, Emma and Mum met us at the beach at the end of the lane.

"How did it go? Did youse win?" Mum asked.

"I don't think Dad wants to talk about it, there was a bit of a shouting match at the end there, let's just get inside and change the subject," I said quickly.

Dad, who was still red in the face, said nothing and marched down to the library, where we heard discordant and angry music that might well have been Bax and Bix.

The next morning I packed for the pilgrimage to Station Island with sleet and hail hammering the windows. It was the first week of March but we were still firmly in the grip of winter. I sat on the window ledge and caught my breath. For the last few weeks I'd been having trouble catching my breath in the mornings. If I wasn't worried about a diagnosis of cancer or emphysema I would have gone to the doctor before this. I'd cut way down on the smokes, maybe it was time to cut them out completely?

"How are you doing, Sean?" Beth asked and before I could answer added: "You shouldn't look so gloomy, I think this will be great for you and your Dad."

"You really want to know how I feel?"

"Is it going to be something positive?"

"I have nothing positive to say. Will you take two negatives?"

"No."

"Jesus, Beth, I really don't want to go on this bloody trip. I only agreed because I thought he'd forget all about it."

"Sean! Phone!" my mum shouted from the living room.

I walked down the hall and picked up the receiver. "Hello?"

"Sean, I'm really sorry to bother you on your holiday."

It was Detective Sergeant McCrabban. I'd recognised his dour, sibilant Ballymena intake of breath before he'd said a word.

"That's OK, Crabbie old son. It's always a pleasure to hear from you."

"How's your trip going?"

"It's all right, Crabbie. It's pouring, but, you know, that's to be anticipated in Donegal. Everything OK there?"

"Yeah, everything's fine."

"So to what do I owe the pleasure of this call?"

"Well, you told me to call you if anything interesting came up."

"And has something interesting come up?" I asked expectantly.

"There's been a murder."

"What sort of a murder?"

"Someone killed a drug dealer."

"Doesn't sound so interesting."

"No, but they killed him with an arrow. Shot him in the back with an arrow, so they did."

"Injuns?"

"Well . . ."

"Or that miscreant from Sherwood Forest who gives the local law enforcement agencies so much difficulty?"

"Here's the bit that I thought might get you intrigued. This is the second drug dealer that's been shot with an arrow in as many days."

"Two drug dealers. Both of them shot with arrows?"

"If you want to be technical about it – and I know you do – they were actually crossbow bolts."

"From the same crossbow?"

"We haven't removed the bolt from the second victim yet. We've only just discovered him."

"I see. And this first guy?"

"He lived."

"Well, that's good. I suppose. Where was he shot?"

"In the back like victim number two."

"Did he happen to see who shot him?"

"Maybe, but it's the usual thing. He's not telling us anything."

"Of course not."

"So do you want to come back for it? Or do you want me and Lawson to handle it? Up to you, Sean, but I thought I'd let you know. Our first murder in nearly a year, and a weird one at that . . ."

I lowered my voice. "Crabbie, just between us, you're a total lifesaver, mate. Have you heard of a thing called St Patrick's Purgatory?"

"No."

"No, why would ya, you big Proddy heretic."

I quickly explained the nature of the pilgrimage and what my dad wanted us to do.

"So you see, Crabbie, if I have to rush back to Carrickfergus to help solve this crossbow-wielding-vigilante-potential-serial-killer case I won't have to go to that bloody island and get verrucae, mildew and trench foot."

Crabbie, however, was not one to shirk off religious obligations lightly. "No," he said reflectively. "I think you should do that thing with your father. It sounds very holy, so it does."

"Crabbie, listen, I'm coming back. Saint Patrick and all the sinners in purgatory can wait."

"All right, I won't let anyone disturb the crime scene till you get there. When do you think that would be?"

"It's a one and a half hour drive back to Carrickfergus. If the baby wasn't in the car with me I'd be there in an hour, but as it is I'll have to leave the wife and kid off first and take it easy on the roads. Be there in an hour and a half. Maybe eighty eight minutes, OK? Anything else going on?"

"Did you hear about John Strong?"

"What about him?"

"He's moving on."

"To the choir invisible?"

"To Assistant Chief Constable."

"Same thing, really. Finally someone we almost like up at command level."

"Aye. And listen, what do you know about Bulgaria?"

"Uhm, decent defence and midfield, lacks imagination up front. Why?"

"I'll explain when you get here. 15 Mountbatten Terrace in Sunnylands Estate," Crabbie said.

"Sunnylands Estate – why am I not surprised? All right, take it easy, mate."

I hung up the phone and went into the kitchen with a downcast look on my face.

"What's the matter, Sean?"

"Mum, Dad, I'm really sorry but I have to go back to Carrickfergus. There's been a murder. Suspected serial killer. Maybe even a vigilante. It's action stations at Carrickfergus RUC. Top brass have been on the phone. The BBC. You know how it is."

"What does this all mean, Sean?" Dad asked.

"I've got to get back. It's all hands on deck. We'll have to do Saint Patrick's Purgatory another time."

I could see the look of relief flit across Dad's face. "Oh dear. Dear oh dear. I'm disappointed, son. I really wanted to go," he lied like a trooper.

"I know, Dad. I wanted to do it, too. We'll just have to go in the summer when the weather's better. Or next year."

"Yes! When the weather's better."

"A murder, Sean? You haven't had one of those for a while," Mum said.

"Nope. This is the first this year. Some drug dealer shot in the back with an arrow."

"Like Saint Sebastian," Mum said sadly.

"Saint Sebastian was shot in the front, love. Several times. You remember the painting by Botticelli," Dad prompted.

"So who am I thinking of that was shot in the back?"

"Jimmy Stewart in *Broken Arrow*? He was shot in the back. *He* survived but poor Debra Paget, his beautiful Apache wife, she died," Dad explained.

"Debra Paget," Mum said thoughtfully.

"She was shot by Will Geer who, of course, went on to play Grandpa Walton," Dad explained.

This was heading the way of all their conversations so I knew

I had to nip it in the bud. I pointed at my watch. "Really sorry about the pilgrimage, Dad. I was so looking forward to it. But someone has to keep the streets safe," I said but neither of them was really listening to me.

"Is Jimmy Stewart still alive?" Mum asked.

"He is too! And in fine fettle. He was on Gay Byrne just last year," Dad insisted.

"Debra Paget, I know that name," Mum said.

"Of course you know Debra Paget!" Dad insisted. "She was Elvis's girlfriend in *Love Me Tender* and she married Chiang Kai-shek's nephew. In real life that is, not in *Love Me Tender*."

"Oh yes, that's right. I remember, now," Mum said, satisfied.

I pointed at my watch again. "Listen, guys, it's been great, but duty calls."

We packed our bags, gave hugs all round and ran outside into the rain.

I looked underneath the BMW for bombs, secured Emma in her car seat and got Beth comfy in the front.

I got in the driver's side, turned the key in the ignition and we both grinned as the Beemer's throaty, fuel-injected six cylinder engine roared into life.

Eighty-eight minutes later I was at the crime scene.

2: JUST ANOTHER DEAD DRUG DEALER

A smallish crowd had gathered in front of 15 Mountbatten Terrace in Sunnylands Estate. No doubt the crowd would have been bigger if it hadn't been raining and this wasn't a Monday. Monday was one of the two signing-on days at the DHSS and more or less everyone in this particular street was either unemployed or on disability and therefore needed to sign on. This had not always been the case. When the Sunnylands Estate had been built in the early 1960s Carrickfergus had three major textile plants and the shipyards in nearby Belfast employed over twenty thousand people. Now the factories had all been closed, the shipyards were down to a rump of 300 men at Harland and Wolff and every scheme the government had tried to bring employment to Northern Ireland had failed miserably. Emigration or joining the police or civil service were your only legitimate options these days. But illegitimate options were to be had joining the paramilitaries and running protection rackets, or if you were a very brave soul you could try your hand at drug dealing.

Independent drug dealers were few and far between because the Protestant and Catholic paramilitaries liked to make an example of them from time to time to show the civilian population that they, not the police, were the ones who could be trusted to "keep the streets safe for the kids". Of course, everyone east of Boston, Massachusetts understood that this was hypocrisy. In a series of agreements worked out at the very highest levels in the mid 1980s the paramilitaries from all sides had effectively divided up Belfast between themselves for the dealing of hash, heroin and speed and the two newest (and most lucrative) drugs in Ireland: ecstasy and crack cocaine.

Such independent drug dealers that there were had to be very discreet or pay through the nose if they didn't want to get killed. Obviously this particular dead drug dealer hadn't been discreet or hadn't paid the local paramilitary chieftain his cut. I'd been thinking about the crossbow bolt in the car. Guns were to be had aplenty for the paramilitaries but a private citizen might have difficulty getting one, which made you think that maybe some kid has a heroin overdose and his dad goes out looking for justice. He can't get a firearm but you get could bows and cross-bows at a sports goods shop . . . Something like that, perhaps?

I parked the BMW and got out of the vehicle. It was a grim little street and it must be truly hell around here in the summer when the only distractions to be had were hassling single women at the bus stop and building bonfires. Frank Sinatra's upbeat "Come Fly with Me" was playing from an open living-room window, but the crowd of about twenty people was sullen and malevolent. I could almost smell the stench of cheap ciggies, unwashed armpits, solvents, lighter fluid and Special Brew. They were mostly unemployed young men who had been drawn away from wanking over page three by a murder on their door-steps. I hated to leave my shiny new BMW 535i sport on a street like this, but what choice did I have?

Several wee muckers came over and began touching the paintwork.

"Get your hands off that," I said.

"Are you a policeman?" a very little girl asked.

"Yes!"

"Where's your gun, then?"

I patted my shoulder holster.

"What type of gun is it?"

"A Glock. A man called Chekov sold it to me. I figure I'll use it at some point." Pearls before swine but hey it's these little things that keep you going. I tried a different one on the girl: "Why don't blind people skydive?"

"Dunno, mister."

"Because it scares the crap out of their dogs."

No smiles at all. I was going to have to go slapstick with this lot and it was too early in the morning for Buster bloody Keaton.

"Is that your car, mister, or did you knock it?" a tall particularly sinister-looking child asked with an unsettling lisp.

"Why aren't you in school, sonny?"

"I got a note from the Royal. I get these terrible headaches. I only go to school when I want to go now," he explained.

"What's your name, son?"

"Stevie, Stevie Unwin," he said and I filed the name away for the future, when the thing in his brain that was giving him the headaches would drive him to the top of a tower with a rifle.

"Mind the car, Stevie, don't let anyone put their paws on it," I said, giving him the customary fiver and began walking towards the crowd. "Step aside there, step aside," I said. The crowd parted reluctantly and with hostility, people muttering highly original things like "bloody peelers" and "bloody cops".

Like Jules Maigret I arrived at the *scène du crime* thoroughly existentially jaded. But lucky old Jules never had a scene like this. The dead drug dealer was lying face down in his front yard, halfway up the garden path. He had orange hair and was wearing a sleeveless denim jacket that said "Slayer" on it in rivets. Under the denim jacket was a bright blue motorcycle jacket. To complete the ensemble he was wearing bleached white jeans and cowboy boots. The crossbow bolt was sticking out of his back, near his left shoulder.

I was surprised to find that the body had not been cordoned off and there was no evidence of forensic men or forensic activity. Indeed, the crowd were so close to the corpse that their cigarette ash was blowing onto the deceased, contaminating the crime scene.

My blood began to boil. In another police force you would have called this chaos. One didn't employ words like "chaos" or "fiasco" to the fine boys of Carrick CID, at least not in my presence, but if this wasn't chaos it could certainly do chaos's job until the real chaos came along in the shape of Ballyclare RUC or Larne RUC or those fuckheads from over the water.

"Everyone get back!" I said, physically pushing some of the onlookers away from the body. "Back there, onto the pavement and put those cigarettes out!"

Where were the forensic officers? And why weren't there uniformed officers on crowd control?

What the hell was happening?

Was this some kind of ambush? No, the spectators would be a lot more cautious if there was about to be a hit. A forensic officer tea break perhaps? That was more likely given their strange ways, but they'd never have buggered off leaving a bunch of eejits dropping cigarette ash over their corpse.

The crowd was nudging up again behind me. "Get back, I said. There's nothing to see here, he won't be doing any tricks, he's not friggin Lazarus."

I examined the victim while the crowd watched me expectantly and Sinatra sang "Chicago", which he did on the British but not the US version of this album. I could take or leave Sinatra, mostly leave, and the record was getting on my nerves. "And somebody turn that effing stereo off!" I yelled and almost immediately the record got yanked with a vinyl-scraping zzzzzippppp!

Now all was silence but for the wind among the crisp packets and shopping bags and the braying of a goat attached by a brick to a piece of rope in the overgrown yard of the house next door that was attempting to reach over said fence and eat the victim's shoelaces. It wasn't getting close but it too was slobbering all over the crime scene.

"And somebody move that goat!" I said.

"And who might you be when you're at home?" a woman asked with an East Belfast accent that sounded like broken glass under a DM boot.

I reached in my pocket for my warrant card but it was back with my bags at Coronation Road.

"Detective Inspector Duffy, Carrick CID," I said flashing my video club membership card in lieu of my police ID.

Suitably impressed, the crowd moved back a little.

I pointed at a likely lad whose Liverpool FC scarf was a sign of above-average intelligence.

"Sonny, do me a favour and move that goat away from the fence," I said.

"What'll I do with it?"

"See that shopping trolley over there filled with bricks? Tie it to that. Here's a quid for a good job," I said.

He grabbed the rope, went next door and tugged the goat away from the body.

"Right! What happened here? Where did the other police officers go?" I asked the crowd, but now everyone was staring at their shoes and saying nowt. The ever present/ever tedious Belfast rule: *whatever you say, say nothing* had come into effect.

"There were other police officers here this morning, where are they now?"

Silence.

The rain increased a fraction and a mist began rolling down the north road from the Antrim Hills. A man on all fours, perhaps with species dysphoria, was attempting to communicate with the goat.

Christ, this was depressing. It didn't help when an ice-cream van pulled up, parked itself at the end of the street and began playing a selection of television themes. Its haunting version of

EastEnders brought a few punters over.

This police/honest-citizen liaison was getting me nowhere. I lit a ciggie and went inside the house where I was met by a distracted and visibly upset Detective Constable Lawson coming down the stairs.

"Oh, sir, thank God you've got here at last!"

"What's going on Lawson? Why isn't my crime scene secured? Where's forensic?"

"I'm so sorry, sir, it's been a bit of a crazy morning. I was just on the phone, I was just trying to call them, I wasn't sure what number, I . . ."

"Call whom?"

"Forensic."

"Surely they were notified by dispatch?"

"Yes, sir. They've been and gone, sir."

"They left?"

"Yes, sir," Lawson said, his lip trembling and his bright blue-green eyes on the verge of tears.

"Are they finished?"

"No. They didn't even get started. Chief Inspector McCann said it was an unsafe work environment. He said it was union regulations."

"What union? What are they . . . Why isn't the victim even covered with a police blanket? He's getting rained on, ashed on and there's little kids staring at him."

"I'm so sorry, sir. I did ask for permission but Inspector Dalziel sort of dismissed my request."

"*Inspector* Dalziel?"

"He got promoted while you were away, sir."

"Let me get this straight. *Inspector* Dalziel arrived from the station and took over the crime scene?"

"Yes, sir."

"And wouldn't let you put a police blanket over the victim?"

"No."

"Why?"

"He said the goat would probably eat it and ruin police property. He may have been being sarcastic, sir, I wasn't sure . . ."

"Why didn't you control the goat, Lawson?"

"I mentioned that as well, sir. I said that the goat was slobbering over the fence, potentially contaminating the crime scene."

"And what did Dalziel say to that?"

"He said that that was forensics's problem. And then he said that the goat was on someone else's property and we'd need permission to enter the house next door to take the goat away from the fence."

"We're the Old Bill. We can do whatever the fuck we want, son!" I said, really angry now.

I noticed that my fists were clenched and my face must have been bright red. Kenny Dalziel had the same effect on everyone he worked with and the bastard was not going to give me a heart attack. I forced myself to take a couple of deep breaths and calm down.

"I'm sorry, sir," Lawson said, all trembly-voiced.

"It's not *your* fault, son. Where the fuck is Sergeant McCrabban? He's supposed to be in charge of—"

"That's what I mean by crazy. I thought you knew, sir. Oh gosh. I thought someone had told you!"

"Told me what?"

"Deauville's wife, sir – Deauville's the victim, sir – she stabbed Sergeant McCrabban when he tried to get her off the body so the forensic officers could do their work."

"Holy shit! Crabbie was stabbed! Why didn't you tell me that straightaway?"

"I thought you knew, sir."

"How would I know? I only just got here. What happened? How is he?"

"Uhm, I was just on the phone with him. Apparently he's fine, sir. No stitches, just a tetanus shot. She stabbed him with a fork.

He didn't want to go to the hospital in the first place but—"

"What happened?"

"Mrs Deauville was very upset. Sergeant McCrabban tried to move her away from the body and she stabbed him in the shoulder with a fork. She's a foreigner, I think. We had to report the stabbing, of course, and, uhm, Inspector Dalziel showed up. He ordered Mrs Deauville placed in custody and he ordered Sergeant McCrabban to report himself to the Royal Victoria Hospital as per the injury-at-work regulations."

"Christ! And then what?"

"And then the forensic team left, saying it was an unsafe work environment."

"And the forensic officer is this McCann fellow, eh? Don't know him. OK. Then what happened?"

"And then I tried to secure the crime scene . . . and the goat . . . and Inspector Dalziel . . ."

I bit my tongue. It wouldn't do to let young Lawson hear my full profanity-laden tirade against a superior officer. "And then Inspector Dalziel left with Mrs Deauville?" I asked.

"Yes, sir."

"Probably the first arrest he's made in years," I couldn't help but mutter.

"Unfortunately Inspector Dalziel took both constables off crowd control to restrain Mrs Deauville in the back of the Land Rover, so that just left me here, sir."

"Are forensic coming back, or what?"

Lawson flipped open his notebook. "Chief Inspector McCann said that with 'police officers being stabbed and with a hostile crowd in front of the house this was not a safe crime scene for his men to do their work', so they were withdrawing until the crime scene was secured."

"Withdrawing to the nearest pub I'll bet."

"I wouldn't know about that, sir."

"So Dalziel left just you to control the crowd, canvas witnesses and conduct an entire murder investigation?"

"Yes, sir. I'm sorry about all this, sir," he said, correctly inter-preting the look of horror on my face. For this was a nearly perfect fuck up – all we needed now was a newspaper reporter or a random inspection by the Chief Constable.

"All right Lawson, we've got to move fast before the press or a local councillor gets here. Go upstairs, get a clean bed sheet if you can find one and cover up the victim's body. I've already taken care of the goat. Once you've done that, get the crowd back onto the pavement and if you are able please urge them to go indoors."

"But how, sir?"

"Shoot someone in the kneecaps every five minutes until the rest get the message?" I suggested.

"Sir."

"Just use your natural authority. I'll call the Royal, check in on Crabbie, call forensic and get a new team down here pronto. Now, go!"

Lawson found a clean sheet in a linen closet and I called the Royal Victoria Hospital. They looked for Crabbie in Casualty but he had already discharged himself and was on his way back to Carrick, which was typical of him. Crabbie was one of the good guys: solid, dour, competent, hardworking, uncomplaining – a thousand men like him and you could do anything: feed the world, build a bridge across the Bering Straits, terraform Mars. There wasn't another like him in Carrick RUC and I'll bet at the Royal he didn't even ask the nurses for high-dose opiates, which is what I would have done. I hung up and called my old mate Frank Payne from forensic and told him about the behaviour of CI McCann, to which he was suitably outraged.

"Kids today, eh, Francis?"

"You can say that again."

"So you'll send a team down pronto?"

"Aye. I'll scratch your back and you scratch my back."

"If you mean I'll owe you a favour, yes. But I'm not going near that hairy back of yours, it's like Mirkwood in there."

"Just hold the fort there, Duffy, and I'll have a team down there in half an hour. Sunnylands Estate?"

"Yeah."

"Fucking nightmare there, is it?"

"Not as bad as some of the estates in these parts. To describe it as a UVF-ridden shithole filled with whores, druggies and scumbags would be ungenerous."

"Aye well, do me a favour and don't let the crime scene get contaminated, eh? I'm just back from an arson in Larne and them boys from Larne RUC were tramping size tens all over the shop."

"Typical. You know what they say, Frank? What's the difference between Larne and a yoghurt?"

"Dunno."

"You leave them both alone for sixty years and the yoghurt will grow a culture."

"Hilarious, Duffy, don't give up the day job."

I hung up with Frank and next I called my boss, Chief Inspector McArthur, explaining to him that we needed half a dozen constables for witness canvassing and crowd management. It was a relatively slow day at Carrick RUC, so he said that that shouldn't be a problem as long as it didn't involve over-time.

"I don't think over-time will be necessary, sir. I'd be surprised if anyone saw anything at all, sir. Not anything they'll admit to us. We should have the canvassing done in an hour or two."

"And how's Sergeant McCrabban? I heard he was attacked?"

"He's already discharged himself, sir."

"I hope he doesn't put a claim in."

"He won't, sir. This is John McCrabban we're talking about here."

Another police officer might have taken three months off

on disability or even sued the station for compensation, but Crabbie wouldn't do either of those things.

"I'm relieved to hear it."

"Sir, I'm also pretty sure Sergeant McCrabban won't be pressing charges so could you please have Mrs Deauville released from the cells and brought up to the CID Incident Room? Maybe have a WPC give her a cup of tea?"

"That's not going to be possible, Duffy."

"Why's that, sir?"

"Inspector Dalziel sent her up to Castlereagh Holding Centre for processing."

"Castlereagh? For a stabbing?"

"Stabbing a police officer."

Dalziel was no doubt cock-a-hoop over his arrest but this wouldn't do at all. If Mrs Deauville was processed at Castlereagh we wouldn't get to interview her for two or three days and as every tedious fuck will tell you, the first forty-eight hours are *the* most important in any criminal investigation.

"Sir, can you do me a favour and patch me into Kelly at the switchboard?"

"Of course, Duffy, see you later."

". . . Switchboard, this is Kelly."

"Kelly, this is Sean Duffy, listen to me, someone's off in a Land Rover taking a Mrs Deauville to Castlereagh Holding Centre. I want you to find out who it is and tell them to come back to Carrick RUC. OK?"

"Yes that's right, Sean, Constable Pollock's driving her up to Castlereagh."

"You get on the blower to Pollock and tell him to turn the Land Rover around and come back to Carrick."

"Sean, this is Inspector Dalziel's arrest," Kelly said dubiously.

"That's OK, I'll deal with Inspector Dalziel. Just get that Land Rover to turn round and return to the barracks."

"OK, Sean, I'll do it but I don't want Inspector Dalziel giving me a hard time."

"He won't. Patch me through to his office will you, Kelly?"

"OK, Sean."

A short pause . . .

"Inspector Kenneth Dalziel, admin, Carrickfergus RUC."

"Dalziel, it's Duffy."

"You finally showed up, did you? I have to tell you, Inspector Duffy, that the competence of your department leaves a lot to be desired. I found a scene of total disarray when I got there," was his opening sally. Dalziel was the son-in-law of a prominent high court judge but that didn't bother me as you knew his father-in-law probably couldn't stand him either.

"Listen to me, Kenny, if you interfere in any future CID investigations or boss around any of my men ever again I am going to come round your house and take that gnome you have with the fishing pole in your front garden and shove gnome and pole up your arse until the wee red hat comes out your bloody throat. Savvy?"

"You can't talk to me that way, Duffy, I've been promoted to—"

"I'll talk to you any way I fucking please, you useless ballbag fuck. Now I'm having Mrs Deauville brought back to Carrick to be questioned and I don't want you to interfere, OK?"

"I'm sending her to Castlereagh to be processed. In my opinion she is a Category 1 offender who needs to be centrally processed: a dead drug-dealer's wife who assaulted a police officer . . ."

"The facts aren't in but don't let that stop you giving your opinion."

"If that Land Rover shows up here, Duffy, I'm sending it back to Castlereagh."

"I dare you. I fucking dare you to do that, Dalziel!" I said and slammed the phone down.

I took a few deep breaths and went back outside.

The body had been covered with a sheet, the goat was being

held back by a kid, but the crowd was even bigger now as we found ourselves in that unhappy window between people returning from their morning dole appointments and daytime TV kicking in. The sky was overcast and drizzling but what I wouldn't give for a short thunder shower to send these gawkers indoors.

Lawson had gone out onto the street and was now locked in a battle of wills with the ice-cream-van driver who had pulled his truck right up in front of the victim's house in the exact place where the forensic team would want to park their Land Rovers. Sensing his youth and low rank, the van driver and the crowd were hassling Lawson with invective extravagant even by the somewhat elevated standards of Sunnylands Estate.

It would never do. I pushed my way through the unwashed mob and told the ice-cream-van driver to fuck off before I arrested him for obstruction.

He could see the fury behind my eyes and like a sensible chap he fucked off back to the end of the street again. Some of the crowd went with him and, satisfied with this momentum, I turned to the others.

"This is a police matter. Get back inside your houses or I'll lift the bloody lot of you!" I said, seething.

A heavy-set red-faced man with a minister's collar got in my face. "I'm the Reverend William McFaul, I'm chairman of the residents' association. How dare you speak to us like that! This is our street and our concern."

"Reverend McFaul, please tell your friends and parishioners to get back inside their homes. There's nothing to see here. These people are obstructing police officers at their work and contaminating a crime scene," I replied.

"We have a right to see what the RUC is doing on our street!" McFaul said, trembling with rage.

"You bloody don't."

"I'm a God-fearing man. I'm not used to such language," McFaul said.

"Language? You mean 'bloody'? Do you also clutch your pearls and occasionally get the vapours? Come on now, move along," I said, pushing him away from the house.

"I'll report you!"

"That's fine but just make sure you do it from the other side of the street," I said, giving him another shove.

"You are an extremely rude young man. What is your name? I am going to call your supervisor," McFaul said, taking a diary and a pencil out of his overcoat pocket.

"My name is Inspector Kenneth Dalziel of Carrickfergus RUC. My supervisor is Chief Inspector McArthur. Report me all you want," I said, giving him a last push and walking back to the crime scene with a feeling of immense satisfaction.

Lawson had found some "RUC CRIME SCENE DO NOT CROSS" tape and was stretching it in front of the house.

"Forensic are on their way," I told him. "Should be here in twenty minutes."

Before Lawson could reply, an old lady in full old lady rig popped out of the throng and began jabbing her finger in my chest. "Is this what it takes for the police to finally come? A murder? I call and call and youse take half the night to get here. It's a disgrace. The kids racing up and down the street, joyriding. Drinking at all hours. Smoking them funny cigarettes. Bad manners to the old folks. The whole country is going to the dogs."

"I quite agree, madam. What's your name?"

"Ivy McAleese," she said.

"Well Mrs McAleese, Constable Lawson here will take your statement," I said. Lawson flipped open his notebook and began writing down the woman's litany of complaints. I listened with interest: kids, drugs, loud music. The old bird didn't know how lucky she had it. She and all the good people of Belfast and the north Belfast suburbs: lucky. These were the good days. Couldn't they see the future? Entropy maximising. Neighbour against neighbour. Blood feud. The disintegration of this lost lonely province into warring camps. *The falcon cannot hear the falconer* . . . And good luck getting the cops then, love. Call 999 and it'll just ring and ring and ring.

But we're not quite down that shit hole yet, are we?

When the old lady had given Lawson a pageful I thanked her for her cooperation and ducked under the police tape with my young colleague and lifted the sheet from the body.

The crossbow bolt had hit the victim close to his left shoulder. There was very little bleeding on the denim jacket around the wound but there was a lot of dried blood on either side of his stomach . . . ergo he'd been shot in the chest first and he'd managed to make a run for it. Run almost up to his front door before they'd shot him again in the back.

"What do you know about what happened, Lawson?"

"Until forensic conclude their inquiries we don't really know anything, sir."

"Who found the body?"

"Mrs Deauville, this morning."

"Where was she last night?"

"In the house, I believe, husband never came home so she went to bed."

I touched the victim's hand. Ice cold. Rigor. Dead about nine or ten hours.

"So he's been here all night too?"

"So I gather, sir, although forensic will confirm that."

"Sergeant McCrabban said on the phone that he was a known drug dealer."

"We ran the victim's ID through the computer and half a dozen arrests came for drugs and drug possession in Bangor and before that London. He's from here originally but he's lived mostly in London, if his charge sheet is to be believed."

"That's why I'd never heard of him. When did he move to Carrick?"

"According to the local residents about four weeks ago."

"Ah so he was the new drug dealer on the block."

"Yes, sir."

"What type of drugs?"

"Sergeant McCrabban had Sergeant Mulvenny go through the house with his canine team."

"Sniffer dogs. Good thinking, that. What did they come up with?"

"Nothing, although Sergeant Mulvenny says Felix got excited."

"Who's Felix?"

"He's the heroin dog."

"Did you find any heroin?"

"No, but Sergeant Mulvenny thinks there may have been some in a couple of empty paint tins at the back of the house."

"So he's moved the drugs off site."

"Yes, sir."

"We'll have to look into that."

"Yes, sir."

"All right, now. Our victim. What do you see in front of you? We don't always have to let forensic tell us everything. We can make a few deductions on our own, can't we?"

"Yes, sir. Uhm, well, the victim's boots are clearly very expensive so he must have been making a lot of money."

I clocked the boots and yes they did look expensive. Snakeskin cowboy boots with flat soles. Slippery flat stoles that must have been a bugger to run in. If he'd been wearing sneakers the poor bastard might have lived.

"What else do you see, Lawson?" I asked, looking into his eager blue eyes. He was still a junior detective but Lawson wasn't like the usual time wasters they gave you to fill out your CID team. Lawson was smart and he had peeler wisdom beyond his years. Sooner or later some git from Belfast would spot his talent and promote him to detective sergeant and poach him away to the fraud squad or Special Branch. Five years from now

– if I was still alive – I'd probably be working for him.

"Not much bleeding from the crossbow bolt, is there?" he said.

"No. There isn't. So what does that tell you?"

"It wasn't the primary wound?"

"Exactly."

"Oh I see, sir. There's blood under the body. So he was shot in the front first, he turned, ran, and then they shot him again in the back?"

"That would certainly be my take. He must be lying on the first bolt, which is in his stomach or chest. You can't really hide a crossbow behind your back as you're walking towards someone, so I'd guess that the assailant was in a vehicle. And unless it was a drive-by (and I've never heard of a crossbow drive-by) Mr Deauville was probably approaching the vehicle, offering to sell them drugs."

Lawson nodded in agreement.

"What else do you see? Tell me about the leather jacket. Where would you get a fancy jacket like that, Lawson?" I asked, feeling the jacket's soft leather sleeve.

Lawson also felt the sleeve. "From Slater and Sons in Glasgow, sir. Three hundred and fifty quid. He liked the style so much he brought two of them. Got a fifty quid discount."

"How did you do that? Some kind of latent paranormal ability?"

"Uh, no, sir, there's a stack of receipts on a spike in his dining room. Had a look through them while we were waiting for you."

"What else did the receipts tell you?"

"Mostly receipts for furniture, white goods and dishware. Stuff you need for moving house."

"What kind of a name is Deauville?"

"Huguenot."

"Tell me everything you got on him."

"According to the rent bill from the housing executive he only moved in on January 15th – that's why we hadn't heard of him yet in Carrick CID, although he has a charge sheet as long as your arm. Robberies, burglaries and it looks like for the last year or two he's been dealing drugs."

"Heroin?"

"Sergeant Mulvenny's dog thinks so."

"How does a brand new drug dealer suddenly break into the heroin trade?"

"Don't know so, sir."

"Enemies?"

"He's not a known player, so I imagine the local paramilitaries here weren't too happy with someone muscling in on their territory. And taking the temperature of the local residents – Mrs McAleese and the minister there – apparently Mr Deauville hadn't gone out of his way to make friends."

"At least his missus was upset at his demise. What did she tell you before she was carted off?"

"Not much, sir."

"Hates the cops, eh?"

"English isn't her mother tongue."

"No need to bring her mother's tongue into the discussion, little too early in the morning for that sort of talk."

"What? Sir, I wasn't trying—"

"I know," I said wearily. "Where's she from?"

"Bulgaria. We couldn't understand anything."

"Bulgaria?"

"Bulgaria."

"How did those two love birds meet?"

"He went on a package trip to the Bulgarian Riviera, sir."

"There's a Bulgarian Riviera?"

"Yes, sir, on the Black Sea coast."

"Didn't know that. Holiday romance?"

"Apparently so, sir. She came back with him last year and they married in September. This according to Bangor RUC."

"And she doesn't speak any English?"

"Not any that she's used with us. How's your Bulgarian, sir?"

"Rusty, I've got to admit. Although it's one of the Romance languages, I think."

"No, sir. You're thinking of Romanian, which has a Latin root. It's a Slavic language."

"OK. Well, without wishing to slight the intellectual capacities of the station I have a feeling we don't have a Slavic speaker on the staff."

"We don't. Already checked, sir."

"So did she say *anything* about what happened?"

"She said plenty. I wrote some of it down."

Lawson flipped open his notebook. "When we arrived she was hugging the body and screaming *obícham te! obícham te!* over and over."

"What do you think that means? Is that his name in Bulgarian, do you think?"

Lawson gave me one of those looks that young people reserve for older people when they wish to convey their patience with the oldster's folly.

"Te is probably the tu form in Bulgarian, wouldn't you say, sir?"

"Oh . . . yes, I'm sure you're right. So she's saying *what happened to you* or *I love you*, or something like that."

"I imagine so, sir."

"Good-looking woman?"

Lawson coloured. "Uhm, I don't know. I suppose if you like that sort of thing, uhm . . ."

"No one is going to accuse you of a lack of gallantry, Lawson. Is she young?"

"Mid twenties, sir."

"Yes, good contact to have if you're dealing heroin. Young, reasonably attractive woman with a Bulgarian passport. Bulgaria is right next to Turkey, I believe, where the emerald fields of marijuana and the scarlet fields of poppy grow in the plentiful Mediterranean sunshine. And of course there's the— Oh shit, that bloody goat again."

The goat was tied to a shopping trolley that had been filled with bricks. There were about thirty bricks in the shopping trolley which probably weighed about forty pounds. If sufficiently motivated the goat could in fact have pulled the shopping trolley behind it and made an admittedly slow escape through the estate. The goat, however, being a goat, was smarter than that and had decided to eat the rope with which it had been tied to the trolley. It had been munching on this rope since we had arrived and presumably for much of the previous couple of days. Escape was now imminent.

"That goat is our only eyewitness, Lawson. Get the tow rope from my car and tie it up properly and when you've done that— Oh my God, here comes our old friend, back from the wars!" I said getting to my feet.

Detective Sergeant McCrabban was getting out of a Land Rover that he'd driven back here himself from the hospital.

I ran over and gave the big galoot a hug, which, of course, horrified him – Crabbie not being the biggest fan of outward shows of affection or human contact.

"Crabbie! It's so bloody good to see you. Jesus, can't I leave you alone for two days without someone trying to kill you?" I said, pumping his hand.

"No one tried to kill me, Sean. Mrs Deauville was just a little upset that I asked her to keep away from the body until the forensic officers came. Where are they, by the way?"

"Came and went mate, like the pack of wankers they are," I said. "Lawson, the goat, please! So how's your shoulder, mate?"

"It's completely fine. No stitches, just a plaster and a tetanus shot. No hard feelings on my part – the woman was clearly distressed. Where is Mrs Deauville, by the way?" Crabbie asked.

I filled him in on the whole sorry business, leaving out my

observations on Kenny Dalziel's competence. " . . . so she's back in Carrick now, but we'll need a Bulgarian speaker if we're going to interrogate her," I said.

"That's going to be tricky, Sean. I've checked. There is no Bulgarian consulate in Northern Ireland. I called up Queens and they don't have anyone on staff who speaks the language – they suggested that we contact the school of Slavic languages in London or the Bulgarian Embassy in Dublin."

"Then that's what we'll do. What about this first victim who you said got shot by this crossbow maniac? What's his name and where's he?"

"Morrison is his name. Unpleasant wee toerag. He's down in Larne hospital. A dozen stitches, lost a bit of blood but he's fine."

"He see anything?"

"He told me he didn't see who shot him and has no idea why anyone would target him."

"But he's definitely a drug dealer too?"

"Oh yes. Eleven convictions for possession over the last five years and he's in the files as a current dealer."

"Was he shot from a car?"

"He quote didn't see anything unquote. And quote, even if I had, I'm no bloody grass, unquote."

"I'll talk to him tomorrow. Him and Mrs Deauville, if we can get a Bulgarian speaker."

Two Land Rovers pulled up and a team of forensic officers got out, led by the grim lardy face of Chief Inspector Payne.

I shook his hand and he shook the hands of Lawson and McCrabban, who he remembered from the sad case of Lily Bigelow.

"Good to see you, Sean. You're looking well . . . for someone twice your age. Is your man going to lynch that goat, Duffy? It looks like a nasty piece of work," Payne said, lighting a ciggie and smoking it with the kind of determination you seldom saw any more in cops under fifty.

"This goat will not be harmed on my watch. He reminds me of me: determined, obstinate, omnivorous. Take him round the back of the house and tie him up, Lawson," I said.

When Lawson had gone Crabbie said in an undertone "It's not a 'he', it's a nanny goat, Sean," which brought a hideous cackle from Payne.

"Duffy thinks of himself as a she-goat. Hilarious!" Payne said.

"Don't you have work to do, mate?"

"Aye I suppose I better get cracking. You lads need to see how a professional does his job."

The crowd-control officers from the police station finally arrived and I gave them a mini seminar on how to canvas for witness statements: no leading questions, keep everything as general as possible and the old who, what, when, where, how. Incredibly and depressingly this was news to most of them.

I let them all get to work and went inside to make some phone calls.

The Bulgarian Embassy in Dublin was very cooperative and said that they would send up a translator and consular representative first thing in the morning.

Payne found me reading the first completely unhelpful statements from Mr Deauville's neighbours in the living room.

"I determined the cause of death," he announced.

"Yes, well, that one didn't exactly take Dr Gideon Fell."

"Who?"

"What did you find out?"

"You plods in CID won't have realised it but your victim was actually shot twice!" he said with unconcealed triumph. "He was shot in the back, of course, but it was a crossbow bolt in the stomach that killed him. It nicked what I believe to be the superior mesenteric vein and he bled to death. Even if he'd made it inside here he would have died."

"Tell me about these crossbow bolts."

"Well, I'm no expert on that, but they look normal to me.

Barbed crossbow bolts for target shooting or hunting. I've got the shoulder one in an evidence bag for you. The pathologist will need to remove the other one."

"Time of death?"

"About one this morning. I'm not going to be more specific than that. The last time we had a case together the medical examiner gave me an awful bollocking for being too specific about the time of death," he said, again recalling the Lily Bigelow case.

"Very good, Francis," I said, shaking his hand again.

"The boys from the morgue are here if you want to give them the nod."

I went outside and gave permission for the body to be removed as I read the last of the witness statements. None of Deauville's neighbours would admit to anything. They didn't really know the deceased, he had kept to himself, they didn't know any of his acquaintances, had never heard of any threats to his life or person.

This was also the bog-standard response to pretty much any murder in Northern Ireland, especially a murder that seemed to have a paramilitary connection. For what seemed like the millionth time in my career I had encountered Belfast's code of omerta that babes must learn at their mother's knee.

I looked at the crossbow bolt in the evidence bag. Didn't seem remarkable but I'd find out more about it.

I put Lawson in charge of a couple of constables to thoroughly search the Deauville residence before Crabbie and I returned to the station in my mercifully unfucked-with Beemer.

Mrs Deauville had been returned to Carrick CID. She was literally spitting with fury and they had put her back in the cells rather than Interview Room 1 where she couldn't wreck the two-way mirror and video-recording equipment. She wasn't bad-looking, if you didn't mind chain-smoking peroxide blondes. I'm a Debbie Harry fan, so, you know . . .

Crabbie and I tried a few questions but she appeared to have only a few stock phrases in English:

"You fucking shit . . . Six pack beer . . . Move your arse, grandma . . . Your clothes shite . . ." which were probably enough to get you through six months of life in Northern Ireland but wouldn't really do in a murder inquiry.

Her name was Elena and even after tea and biscuits she was visibly upset so I sent down a brave WPC to comfort her with a blanket and more tea and biscuits.

"How do we know she didn't do it?" I asked Crabbie. "She has a temper."

"No sign of a crossbow in the house."

"She shoots her husband and throws the murder weapon in the sea?"

"And leaves his body outside the house all night?"

"She was drunk when she did it. Wakes up this morning. Oh my God, what have I done? Calls the cops, gets the waterworks going."

"Why would she do it?"

"They had a fight? He was having an affair?"

"She seemed genuinely upset to me."

"Remorse?"

"Maybe," Crabbie conceded. "But we didn't find a receipt for a crossbow in the house."

"Who keeps receipts? Oh wait, he does. Still, let's bring a picture of Deauville and his wife to every shop selling crossbows in Ulster. If the shopkeeps recognise either of them we probably are dealing with a domestic," I said.

"You could be right. But then there's the other case."

"The other case, yes, damn it."

I made some more phone calls. Special Branch informed me that there was indeed a vigilante group called Direct Action Against Drug Dealers (DAADD) who occasionally killed drug dealers in Belfast and environs. DAADD, of course, was just one of many cover names for the IRA and its offshoots and splinter groups.

"If this was a DAADD killing they probably would have already claimed it so they could make the evening news. They're very media savvy," Trevor Finlay from Special Branch intel informed me.

"We haven't had any claims of responsibility, yet," I told him.

"Nor us."

"Meaning?"

"Might not be DAADD. Unlikely they would drive all the way up to Carrickfergus, anyway. If I was to guess, Sean, I'd say that this was something else."

"Thanks, Trevor."

I called up Roy Taylor in statistics and he told me that there had been twelve deaths by crossbow in the last thirty years, all of them manslaughters or non-prosecutable accidents.

I found out that there were two shops in Northern Ireland that sold crossbows. Both in Belfast. I called both and was told the rather disheartening information that they had sold over two hundred crossbows each in the last year. The shops were not legally obliged to keep the names and addresses of their buyers and none had. I gave them the make and serial number of the bolt in the evidence bag and unfortunately this was the most common type of crossbow bolt. Tens of thousands of them were sold in Europe every year.

Around five o'clock Lawson came back with the PCs from the house and area search. The house, rubbish bins, Mill Stream and skip search had revealed no dumped crossbow. The house search had revealed no more drugs or useful enemies list or even more useful address book but Lawson had found about a thousand quid in a paper bag under the oven and an old .455 Webley semi automatic pistol that had to be fifty years old if it was a day.

"This thing's an antique," Crabbie said, impressed.

"It looks like he never cleaned the mechanism, I doubt it would even fire," I replied.

"Should we take it to the range and find out?" Lawson suggested eagerly.

Crabbie and I shook our heads together. The dodgy-looking old thing would probably explode in our hands and Carrick CID had suffered enough today.

"Oh go on, sir," Lawson pleaded.

"We take that down the range, it misfires and gets me right in the kisser."

"You're a glass-half-empty kind of guy, sir, aren't you?"

"I don't even acknowledge the existence of the glass, son."

Crabbie nodded at the forbidding wisdom of this remark.

I yawned. "It's getting late. Case conference tomorrow morning, you lads can go home. First order of business on the morrow will be to question the wife," I said.

I typed up a brief summary of all that we knew and closed my eyes for a bit in my recliner. I must have gone straight out because I heard a voice from deep, deep in the well ask "Is he asleep, do you think? Can we nudge him?"

"Speak Lord! Thy servant heareth!" I said and opened my eyes on Constables Collins and Fletcher. "Oh it's you two. What do you want?"

"The Chief Inspector wants a progress—"

"Tell him I'll be there in two minutes. Just enough time for him to get the good whisky out of its hiding place in the bottom shelf of his filing cabinet."

I gathered my thoughts, ran a hand through my hair and went into the Chief Inspector's office to give him my formal summary of the day's events.

Chief Inspector McArthur had been our gaffer for three years now and the disappointment was beginning to show on all sides. A Scot who'd been trained at the police college in Hendon, he was a high flyer who'd probably expected to be done with his rotation in Carrickfergus RUC in about eighteen months before getting a promotion to Superintendent and a move to somewhere more interesting. It hadn't happened and I sometimes wondered if he blamed me and my bad voodoo for his career doldrums.

"Ah, Duffy, have a seat. Whisky?"

For a while the Chief Inspector and I had been on collegial first-name terms but now it was mysteriously back to "Duffy". Had I done something wrong? Already? I'd only been back from my hols a few hours.

"No thank you, sir, Beth hates it when I come home from duty with whisky on my breath," I said.

"Yes, she's right, I suppose we all should cut down on—"

"But if you insist, sir, just two fingers of that sixteen-year-old Jura would hit the spot about now."

He made me a Jura and poured a Johnny Walker and soda for himself and I sat down opposite. He read my report while I examined him. He was a boyish-looking thirty-five or thirty-six, with no grey hair that I could see in his elegantly parted locks. I dug his Top Man black suit too. Nice cut, nice lines and if I'd been fifteen years younger and liked suits or him I'd of asked him about it.

"Before we begin I should let you know, Duffy, that Inspector Dalziel is thinking of writing up a formal complaint about you."

"Is he now?"

"Yes. I tried to talk him out of it, but he's pretty adamant. Says you were rude to him over the phone. Make it go away, Duffy, eh? Apologise to him, OK?"

"Yes, sir, I'll take care of it, sir."

"Changing the subject: your team did all those blood tests we asked for last week, didn't they?"

"Yes, sir. For the annual fitness thing? Is that coming up soon, sir?"

"I shouldn't really say, Duffy, but I can tell you that we're doing things very differently this year. We're taking officer fitness much more seriously."

"I know. I'm always telling the men that, sir. My crew is as fit as a fiddle and I'm a model of health myself, sir. I'm just back from Donegal; you know what it's like out there: walking on the beach, hiking in the woods, mountain-climbing, swimming."

He lowered his voice and leaned forward conspiratorially. "Hmmm, yes, well, make sure you and all your team are here at the station tomorrow, I've heard a rumour that Chief Superintendent Strong is coming in."

"Really? So it is tomorrow, is it? The fitness test thing?"

"You didn't hear that from me but just make sure you and all your team are at the station in the morning and they don't go on the piss tonight."

"Crack of dawn, we'll be here."

"Good," McArthur said finally skimming through the report. "So you've gotten a murder case, Duffy?"

"Yes, sir."

"In Sunnylands Estate, it says here. I went there once. Its distinguishing features seemed to be religious bigotry, cockfighting and despair."

"Cockfighting?"

"So I imagine, or perhaps dog-fighting. Unsavoury place. Residents looked deranged and desperate to escape. Afraid to drive my Merc through it and I certainly wouldn't park it there."

"No, sir."

He slid the report back across the desk. "All seems to be in order here, Duffy. I take it you are not going to ask for additional resources on this one or, God forbid, over-time?"

"Too early to say, sir. The case could go in any number of directions."

He frowned. "Well, there's no point going overboard is there?"

"Why's that, sir?"

"It's just another dead drug dealer, isn't it? No family, wife's a foreigner, he's a bloody repeat offender. You know what everyone's going to say around here: good riddance. Pardon my language, Duffy, but who's going to give a damn about him?"

I looked at the Chief Inspector for an uncomfortable five seconds. This kind of talk annoyed me no end.

"*I* am going to give a damn about him, sir. *My men* are going to give a damn about him. *Carrick CID* is going to give a damn about him," I said and with the rule of threes ringing in his skull I finished the whisky, set the glass down on his desk, and exited the office with enough fizzy melodrama to have made the heart of the octogenarian Bette Davis in far-off California skip a beat.

I was still grinning when I made it back to Coronation Road ten minutes later.

3: THE BIG SHEEP

"What are you so pleased about?" Beth asked as I waltzed through the door kissing girlfriend, baby girl and cat, in that order.

"Oh nothing. Just something I said to the Chief Inspector."

"Is that whisky on your breath? You know I worry about you driving with the liquor in you."

"The Chief Inspector was pouring so it barely covered the bottom of the glass."

She handed me a cold can of Bass. I popped it and took a gulp. A cigarette would have gone down well here but I was limiting myself to half a pack a day and I only had two left to get through the night.

"How was the cat in our absence?"

"He's fine, but Niamh overfed him. She gave him two tins a day."

I stroked him on the head again. He was a long, lean cat who burned off a lot of energy. "He looks OK to me."

"How's your big case?" Beth asked.

"It's a murder all right. Some lunatic going around shooting drug dealers with a crossbow."

"Will you be able to solve it?"

"I very much doubt it. No eye witnesses either because there were no eye witnesses or because they think the paramilitaries killed him and everyone is afraid to blab. Add in the fact that the murder weapon is an extremely common piece of equipment and that Mr Deauville was a drug dealer so he had many enemies and rivals . . . Nope it's not looking good for a resolution."

"And yet you seem cheerful enough?"

"Well we'll give it the old college try, won't we? You know how many murder cases I've successfully brought to trial since moving to Carrickfergus?"

"How many?"

"Zero."

"And again you're smiling, what's up with you, Sean?"

I pulled her close and got a whiff of her perfume. I brushed a line of red hair from her forehead and kissed her on the lips.

"A man's nothing without a purpose. For the last couple of months we've been treading water but now I've got something solid to work on and by God I'm going to work on it no matter what that idiot Chief Inspector has to say about it."

"You want a purpose? Change Emma and take her for a walk before the rain comes on again. Dinner will be up in half an hour."

"OK."

When I changed Emma's nappy and powdered her she fell asleep on the changing table so I transferred her to the cot.

"OK to let her nap?" I called into Beth.

"Yeah, that's fine. Hey, Niamh told me a joke. What do you get when you cross an agnostic, a dyslexic, and an insomniac?"

"Uhm—"

"An eejit who stays up all night wondering if there really is a dog," I said.

I smiled and went out to the shed to "work on rebuilding my Triumph Bonneville", a fiction Beth and I both accepted.

Shed.

Paint tins.

I had no idea sniffer dogs had gotten so sensitive so I moved my stash out of said tins and put it in a block of engine grease.

I picked up the extension phone and called Johnny Freeman, my marijuana dealer.

"Hello?"

"What's that noise in the background. Is someone murdering cats?" I asked.

"It's Kylie Minogue, as you well know."

"I suppose you heard the news."

"Of course. It was all over the *Daily Mirror*. Ian Rush is unhappy at Juventus and would love to come back to Anfield."

"Not that news. What do you know about this dead drug dealer?"

"Oh, him? Unaffiliated independent operator. Only a matter of time before he got kneecapped or topped or threatened with kneecapping and topping."

"You don't sound particularly worried, Johnny."

"I pay for protection. Twenty per cent. And still my prices cannot be beat in all of East Antrim . . . Did the drug squad seize any merchandise?"

"Nope. Nothing in the house. He must have a lock-up somewhere."

"And when you find the lock-up?"

"Everything will be under lock and key in the property room. Weighed and catalogued. Destined to remain there until the investigation is concluded. This is a murder case."

"What do they do with narcotics evidence after the case is over?"

"They destroy it."

"*Who* destroys it?"

"Forget it, Johnny. There's a whole procedure for illicit goods. A team from Belfast will come down for it and they'll take it with them and then it'll be incinerated."

"Crying shame."

"Johnny, if I could bring you back to the matter in hand. A man's been murdered here. What do you know about Deauville?"

"Nothing. Moved here from Bangor a few months ago. Worked out of Sunnylands and Castlemara. Not my turf, so I didn't care."

"Whose turf was it?"

"The UVF runs them estates, as you well know."

"Why would they kill him?"

"Because he wouldn't pay a percentage?"

"Why wouldn't he pay a percentage?"

"Because he's an idiot? I don't know."

"They shot him with a crossbow."

"Yeah I heard that."

"Why would they do that, do you think, when there are plenty of guns floating around?"

"I don't know. Aren't you the detective?"

"Helpful as usual, Johnny. Keep your head down. Bye."

"Bye, Sean and if you can somehow get your paws on any seized gear, I'd—"

I hung up before he could complete the sentence.

I went back inside the house.

"Have I got ten minutes before dinner? Want to return a video," I said.

"Yeah. It's risotto. You like my risotto, don't you?"

"Of course I do, back in ten."

I walked down the street to Bobby Cameron's house and rang his doorbell.

"What do you want, Duffy?"

"Did you hear about the killing today?"

"Aye I did. Drug dealer, no one'll miss him."

"If I wanted to ask if the late Mr Deauville had been paying for protection who would I go see?"

"I'm not telling you that."

I held up the video. "Would it help if I returned this video?" I asked.

Bobby nodded. "It might," he said and shut the door.

*

I checked under the Beemer for mercury tilt switch bombs and drove to Video Extra on the Clipperstown Road.

I went inside with a copy of *Reds* that I hadn't watched and therefore didn't need to rewind.

"How was it?" Andy Young asked. "Not much of a Warren Beatty fan myself."

AKA: Big Andy Young. Andy Mad Dog Young. Andy King Rat Young.

Andy was the UVF deputy Chief of Staff for Carrickfergus and the person in charge of making sure businesses paid their protection money every week. If they didn't it was a brick through the window and if that didn't convince them it was the old Lagan Valley Lightning: a petrol bomb through the window . . .

"Never watched it," I said, putting the video on the counter.

"You might as well keep it. We're changing the whole shop to VHS. Everyone is."

"What will I do with my Phillips recorder?"

"Get rid of it. The format wars are over. Sony won."

"Phillips is a superior system. You can record on both sides," I said, somewhat miffed – that Phillips video recorder had cost me 500 quid.

"Doesn't matter. VHS is the industry standard now and will be until laser discs take over."

"Five years ago they said CDs were going to kill vinyl."

"They did."

"No they didn't CDs are . . . listen Andy, I'm not really here to talk about video recorders and CDs."

"I know."

"How do you know?"

"Bobby Cameron phoned me and told me you were noseying around asking questions."

"It's about this man Deauville."

"What about him?"

"Somebody shot him."

"I heard."

"It wasn't you by any chance, was it?" I asked.

Big Andy's thick white neck swivelled towards me. His eyes were narrow black slits in a menacing blue-white visage that almost looked like a human face.

"I'm no informer, Duffy."

"I know you're not. I'm not suggesting that you are."

"What are you suggesting?"

"I'm wondering why Deauville wouldn't pay protection money when he knew that he was likely to be kneecapped or worse."

"Who says he wasn't paying protection money?"

"Well he was shot, wasn't he?"

Andy shrugged and looked at the TV monitor which was playing *Jaws: The Revenge*.

"Wait a second. Are you saying he *was* paying protection money?"

"I'm not saying anything. I'm no grass," he said, never taking his eyes from the monitor.

The sound was off but a wet Michael Caine was yelling something. Probably something about a shark.

"If you keep watching, Inspector Duffy, you'll see a different ending from the cinema release. The shark blows up, just like in the first one," Andy said.

"Andy, I don't want to seem dense, but are you implying that Deauville was paying protection right enough?"

He looked at me again. "I'm not saying he was, I'm not saying he wasn't. I have no idea."

"If the Inland Revenue investigators were to inspect your business here, Andy, would everything be above board, do you think?"

"You wouldn't. We have a good relationship you and me. I

never make you pay the rewind fees."

"It's all moot anyway if you're only going to be renting VHS
. . . Now tell me plain, was Deauville paying for protection or
not?"

Andy checked to see that there was no one else in the shop
but it was *EastEnders* time so everyone was home watching
telly. He lowered his voice anyway.

"He paid protection."

"So you had no incentive to kill him?"

"No."

"This wasn't a sanctioned hit?"

"He wasn't killed by Carrick UVF or Carrick UDA."

"The local paramilitaries had nothing to do with it?"

"As far as I know, no."

"Cheers, Andy, you've been very helpful."

"No I haven't. I've told you nothing, remember that Duffy."

"You've told me nothing, check."

Back to Coronation Road in time for dinner. Risotto. Apple
crumble and custard for dessert. Two of my favourites. Beth
must be up to something. I did the dishes, made two mugs of
tea and joined her in the living room. The TV was off, the fire
was lit, the record player was on (Schubert by the sound of it).
I picked up my copy of *The Times*, which I hadn't had a chance
to skim through. Beth was reading a book called *Ubik*, but without much obvious enthusiasm. She was looking at me when she
thought I wasn't looking. Yeah, something was going on.

"You have a good day today?" I asked.

"Yes."

"Anything new or out of the ordinary?"

"No. Played with Emma, did some reading."

"Are you at the writing stage of your thesis yet?"

"No, no, lot of reading to do yet."

"Well if you need help with the typing . . . I'm practically a
touch typist now. Fifteen years in the cops will do that for you."

"Thanks, Sean," she said and looked at me again under that adorable ginger fringe.

"So nothing else happened today?" I asked.

"Well . . ."

Here it comes . . .

"Yes?"

"My father called."

"On the phone?"

"No, he came round."

"Really? I'm sorry I missed him. Your mum with him?"

"No, she had her bridge morning."

"What did he want?"

Another evasive look. "He just wanted to see the baby . . . uhm that's all."

The end of Symphony #2.

Empty grooves in the vinyl.

Silence.

The lovely opening of Symphony #3 that Schubert wrote when he was only eighteen years old, a few weeks after the Battle of Waterloo.

"Is that a clarinet?" Beth asked – an obvious ploy to distract me, that worked like a bloody charm.

"Yes. Solo clarinet. Pretty, isn't it?"

"It's good music to have in the background I'll admit that . . . oh there's Emma . . ."

"I'll take care of her."

Upstairs. Change the baby. Downstairs. Baby to Beth for a feed while I did *The Times* cryptic crossword.

Everything going great until the very first down clue "an often mature ham at the local church hall perhaps? (7)" which I fussed over ridiculously so that my completion time came in at a shocking nine minutes. The answer to the clue, of course, was "amateur". "Mature" being a pseudo anagram of "amateur" and "ham" an unkind phrase for a poor actor. I didn't get it because

I didn't realise until halfway through the crossword that more than half the clues were theatre-related.

We turned on the telly and caught the Season 3 premiere of *Miami Vice* – a show all the young cops down the station were raving about but which I'd never seen.

Liam Neeson was in it, playing a reformed IRA terrorist who wasn't as reformed as he made out.

At 9pm I called the station and asked to be put through to the duty officer.

"Carrick CID, this is DC Lawson speaking."

"Thought I sent you home."

"I came back. I'm still duty officer. Unless you want to come in, sir?"

"No, I don't. Any word on the results on our victim?"

"I have them in front of me, sir. They faxed them through an hour ago. It must have been a light day at the M.E."

"Tell me the salients."

"Time of death: between 1 and 2 this morning. Cause of death: haemorrhaging of the superior mesenteric vein."

"Anything unusual?"

"Nope. It's what we were expecting. He'd been drinking but he wasn't drunk and we're waiting for the full narcotics results."

"Was there any sign of any previous beatings, kneecappings, anything like that?"

Lawson ruffled through the report. "Nope. His body was in good shape."

"Strange that they would kill him straight away, isn't it? Usually they'll give you a good punishment beating to make you pay up. Dead men don't pay anything."

"Yes, sir. But a killing can be useful too. The old Voltaire rule."

"The old Voltaire rule indeed." (*Dans ce pays-ci, il est bon de tuer de temps en temps un admiral pour encourager les autres.*)

"How's Mrs Deauville holding up?"

"I don't know. I haven't been down to see."

"Jesus, Lawson, she's our responsibility. CID, not the station. Take her down a clean sheet and a pillow and get her some food."

"Yes, sir. Right away, sir. "

"Goodnight, Lawson. Oh wait, one more thing. I have a feeling the annual fitness test is going to be tomorrow, so if you want to call in sick this would be the day to do it."

"Nice wee run along the seafront. I'd quite enjoy doing it, sir."

"You would. Well, I'm going to have to get Crabbie and me out of it somehow. And I'm dreading getting the results of our blood work the nurse took. All right, fine, goodnight, Lawson."

"Night, sir."

"Oh, before you go, I saw that programme you've all been raving about."

"*Red Dwarf*?"

"*Miami Vice*. Liam Neeson was in it."

"Oh don't tell me anything about it! Me dad's taping it for me. Did you like the cars? Now that they've gotten rid of the kit cars the cars are pretty cool. Cool clothes, too. I wish you'd let me wear a jacket and T-shirt. It's much more practical if you think about it, sir."

"Goodnight, Lawson," I said and hung up.

I went out to the shed, lit a joint and put Robert Plant's *Now and Zen* in the tape player. On one of the songs there was a sample of Kylie Minogue's "I Should Be So Lucky". Was that co-opting or surrender?

I called up Kenny Dalziel at his house but the phone just rang and rang. I'd apologise to the useless cunt tomorrow.

I switched the music off and looked at the stars. The Great Bear rotating slowly and comfortably across the winter sky.

Joint finished I walked back in.

Beth was upstairs getting ready for bed.

She had left her handbag on the kitchen table and neatly folded away inside it was an ordnance survey map of the

Ballypollard Road in the townland behind Magheramorne. I knew that road and that townland.

Beth had circled a field on the Ballypollard Road for reasons best known to herself. What could this be about? Something to do with her father's visit? It was mysterious but there was no percentage in asking her about it because she would know I'd gone into her bag and looked at her stuff. If I recalled correctly the Ballypollard Road had nothing on it at all except for the Ballypollard Wool Shop, which was something of a local landmark because of the giant sheep statue out the front. "The biggest sheep statue in all of Ireland", they claimed. The circle Beth had drawn on the map was about half a mile up the road from the Big Sheep itself, so it wasn't a wool-buying expedition.

I looked at the map until Beth called down to me to ask if I was ever "coming up to bed?"

It had been a long day but I couldn't sleep and although it wasn't my shift I got up to feed Emma at just after two. She fell asleep at the half-bottle mark and I burped her over my shoulder.

Jet the cat was sleeping in front of the paraffin heater but when he saw that I was awake he jumped onto the baby's changing table and rubbed himself against me.

"You're awake too, eh, cat? The two men can't sleep and the two women are out for the count. What's their secret, do you think?"

Jet kept his own counsel while the 9th-century Irish poem *Pangur Bán* floated into my consciousness; I extemporised a translation that would, I think, have pleased Sedulius Scottus himself, even if not my literal-minded fifth-form Irish teacher, Dr Monroe.

How happy we are together, scholar and cat,
Each has his own work, be it study or stalking a rat.
Your shining eyes watch the ratholes, my failing eyes read verse,

I rejoice over logic problems, you over besting your rodent adversaries.

We are pleased with our own methods and neither hinders the other,

Thus we live without tedium or envy, Pangur my brother.

And yes I *was* pleased with my method. It had been a good day professionally and otherwise, but I knew that the good days were the exception and as Noel Coward wisely reminds us, bad times are just around the corner . . .

4: A PRETTY SHITTY MORNING ON THE BALLYPOLLARD ROAD

Voices and meows downstairs. "Sssshhh the pair of you. Daddy is still up there sleeping." *So I'm the father of the cat now too, am I?*

Yeah, I supposed I was. Rescued that cat from almost certain death in England.

I opened my eyes, embraced the light of day.

What a day. Friday the 4th of March 1988.

When I was twelve years old a gypsy boy cursed me when I stopped him from stealing my bike parked outside the pet shop in Buncrana. Nothing had happened at the time, but at the end of Friday the 4th of March 1988 when I put my head down on the pillow at two in the morning I suddenly remembered that evil-faced kid and wondered if maybe his spell had merely been delayed for twenty-five years or so.

But I didn't know that then, snuggled up in the blanket with footsteps coming along the landing.

Beth had brought me a mug of coffee and marmalade on toast.

"What's this in aid of?" I asked suspiciously.

"God, you're so cynical," she said and flounced off making me even more suspicious but also affording me a view of her fantastic bum.

Bum. Coffee. Toast. Not the worst way to start the morning. I flipped on the clock radio.

The nurses were on strike, the ferry workers were on strike and the Birmingham Six had lost another appeal against their convictions even though it was obvious to every peeler in the British Isles that they had been fitted up by the West Midlands Constabulary.

Coffee and toast done I got out of bed and looked through the window across Coronation Road to the Antrim Hills where it appeared to be flurrying.

"Was there snow in the forecast?" I shouted downstairs.

"It's only a light dusting. We'll still be able to drive," she shouted back up.

"We? Are we going somewhere?"

"What time do you have to go into work?"

"I need to be there soonish. Ten at the latest. We're supposed to be having a Bulgarian translator come up from Dublin."

"Ten? Oh we've got plenty of time then."

"Plenty of time for what?"

"Oh, just a little run in the country. I'll drive if you don't want to."

"I don't like the sound of this."

"Live a little, Sean."

"What will we do with Emma?"

"Take her with us."

"Are we going somewhere specific?"

"It's a surprise."

"Now I definitely do not like the sound of it," I muttered to myself.

I showered and dressed in jeans, DM boots, blue shirt, black sweater.

I went downstairs to find Emma and Beth in coats and sweaters all set to go.

"Wait here, let me check under the car first," I said.

I went out to the BMW and checked underneath it for bombs. No bombs but I'd always keep checking. As a student I'd listened to an aged Bertrand Russell's thoughts on the fate of turkeys being fattened for Christmas, the turkeys subscribed to the philosophy of inductivist reasoning and didn't see doomsday coming. I will.

Wife and child came out to the car. Cat staring at us anxiously through the living room window.

"I'll drive," Beth said which meant that we'd be listening to Radio 1 for the entire journey. I mentally prepared myself for an assault of Aswad, Bros, Tiffany, The Pet Shop Boys and Kylie.

"OK, you can drive, but easy on the clutch, please, this is a precision piece of machinery."

She turned the ignition and the magical mystery tour began with a trip down Victoria Road and a turn left onto the Larne Road. We kept on the Larne Road past Whitehead and on to Magheramorne

My worst musical fears were realised when they played three Phil Collins songs in a row. I made a mental note to have Collins's drum solos taped and piped into the interrogation rooms when difficult sods were cooling their heels.

"This is where we turn," Beth said, pulling the Beemer up the Ballypollard Road. Beth and even Emma started singing along to a song called "Joe Le Taxi", which chipped away at the blackness in my hard heart.

"You know you haven't had a single cigarette today?" Beth said happily as we drove deeper in the hills.

"I know, I'm bloody gasping for one," I said.

"The reason why you're gasping is because of the cigarettes, you'll see," Beth said with such uncanny prescience that a few hours later when the RUC doctor was threatening to sign me "unfit for duty" I would wonder briefly if she had the Sight.

"Wind the window down, look at the view," Beth said.

I did as I was bid. We were in a beautiful part of County

Antrim overlooking the North Channel and a big chunk of Western Scotland.

"Where are we going?"

"Have you ever been up here before?"

"I was once at that Big Sheep place where they have the jumpers."

"Yeah, we're not going as far as that. Just a wee bit further now," Beth said.

Beth and Emma sang along to the hits on BBC, I grew more nervous and more in need of a cigarette.

Finally she pulled the BMW along a lane I hadn't noticed before and stopped at a muddy field filled with half a dozen workmen. The field backed onto a little wood and beyond that lay a hamlet, a river and another wood. In the distance you could see all of Islandmagee jutting like a thumb into the water and because it was a clear day the Ayrshire coast of Scotland looked close enough to touch.

I looked at Beth. "What is this?"

"This is our new home," she said with a happy grin on her face which told me that she wasn't kidding.

"What are you talking about?"

"I've told you that I don't want to live in Victoria Estate."

"I know and I said when work eased off I'd take a few weeks and help you look for a place."

"Daddy was over yesterday and I was telling him how much I hated living in Carrick and he said that we could help him out. He's building a house and he wants it to be a model home for a dozen more that will be scattered over parcels of land he has up here. And he said that we could live in it as long as we wanted. A present for us and for the new baby. Here, let me introduce you to Vaughn, the site manager. He'll tell you all about it."

I put Emma on my shoulders to keep her out of the muck and shook hands with Vaughn, a lanky fellow with curly brown hair and likeable brown eyes. Vaughn told me all about it. A four-bedroom house on a nine-acre plot with access to woods and a riding trail. There were two bathrooms, a children's play-room, a library and a stable block.

"We could have horses, Sean!"

"It's good horse country," Vaughn said with the kind of wistful look in his eye that told me he was probably a Catholic.

I took her to one side. "What's going on, Beth?"

Her eyes narrowed. "A house for us. Away from the bloody north Belfast suburbs and those people on Coronation Road."

"Those awful people are my friends."

"You're delusional, Sean. They're not your friends. They hate you because you're a Catholic and because you're a peeler."

"I don't think that's true. Not any more."

"And they certainly hate me. I hear them gossiping about me behind my back. It's awful."

"This is some kind of class thing, isn't it? Some kind of crazy Protestant class thing."

"No! Don't you know anything about me? I'm not that sort at all. I don't care that they're working class or whatever it is they are. I just don't like them. They're rude to me behind my back and I'm lonely."

"Lonely! What do you think you'll be out here? This is the middle of fucking nowhere."

"Sean, please, not in front of the baby."

"Sorry . . . Look, I don't understand you. I wanted to marry you. You turned me down and told me never to bring it up again. Now you want us to move into Barbie's fucking – sorry – Dream House complete with bloody stables. Bit of a mixed fucking message, isn't it?"

She took Emma off my shoulders and held her. The wee lass was looking at the pair of us with bafflement in her big blue eyes. She had never seen us fight before. I had not allowed that to happen.

Beth poked me in the chest. It was unusual for her to get

physical. She must be really worked up.

"What don't you understand, Sean? Dad is giving us this house! To live in as long as we want! Who would turn that down?"

"We already have a bloody house!"

"A house I hate!"

"Aye, let's talk about hate. Your father can't fucking stand me. A Catholic peeler shacking up with his daughter! Jesus Christ I might as well as be Beelzebub himself."

"That's nonsense!"

"Is it? You want to talk about dirty looks, muttering behind backs? You don't know the half of it, love. In the old days he'd of had me horsewhipped."

"Oh my God, you are so dramatic! Listen to yourself!"

"He wants you up here because you'll only be a ten-minute drive away from them in Larne whereas I'll be all the way up in Carrick or in Belfast. No more nipping home at lunchtime to see the bairn. Leaving early in the morning, coming back late at night. Or is that what you want?"

She put her hands on her hips. "Only you, Sean Duffy, only you would react like this when someone is practically giving you a house for free! Only you. You'd cut off your nose to spite your face, you would."

"Free? Nothing's free."

"This is. No strings. It's the show house and we can live here as long as we like. I know Dad, it's his way of giving it to us forever."

"I'm happy where I'm living now. I know people. They know me. You know how hard it was to win them over?"

"You won't have to win anyone over here, Sean. It's a house in the country. Land. There's woods. Think of Emma. Think how happy she'll be. You'll be happy too, I promise."

I could see that she was trying now.

I was being the arsehole and she was trying.

"If Adam and Eve can't make it in Paradise, how are we going to make it in bloody Carrickfergus?" she said with a smile.

"You seriously think I could live here, and be beholden to your father?"

She bit her lip in that gorgeous way of hers and nodded. "That's what it boils down to, doesn't it? It's not him that hates you. It's you that hates him. Some older guy knocks up his daughter and is barely civil to him and he hasn't said one bad word to you. Not one."

"He doesn't need to say anything—"

"He drives a Jaguar and he reads the *Daily Telegraph* and so you've got this picture of him in your head that he's this fucking Colonel Blimp at the golf club who hates your 'fenian guts'. I don't know who that is, but that's not my dad! He's been nothing but civil to you, and now he's giving us a house . . . This is you, Sean. You. You . . ." she said and putting her hands over Emma's ears added "You fucking ingrate."

"I'm an ingrate? I didn't ask for this fucking house! I didn't ask your fucking father to stick his oar into my family business!"

"Is that the way you see it?"

"Aye, that's the way I fucking see it!"

She stomped over to the BMW. She put Emma in the car seat and secured her seat belt, then she got in the driver's seat in the front.

I walked over to the car and tapped the window. "So what now? You're going to fucking drive off dramatically and leave me here?"

The BMW spun its wheels in the mud and I stepped away from the splatter.

The front wheels found some grip and Beth drove out of the field and back onto the lane. I thought, for a moment, about chasing them but there's seldom anything more ridiculous to be seen than a man angrily chasing after fleeing missus.

And chasing her across a slippery muddy field would more or

less invite an encounter with the sheugh.

I looked at the blue line of exhaust smoke curling into the air like a djinn from a bottle. I heard the Beemer shift through the gears on cue until it reached the overdrive on the Ballypollard Road. She hadn't been easy with the clutch.

I walked over to Vaughn, who'd been staring fixedly at the mud during all this time.

I cleared my throat. "Horse country, eh? What type of horses? Hunters, you think?"

"Oh yes, you could stretch a hunter out here," he said.

Definitely a Catholic.

"So how long will this house take?"

Vaughn rubbed his chin. "It depends."

"On what?"

"Well, the blueprints are done and we're in today looking at the drainage. The site drains beautifully, by the way. But we'll need to get planning permission for a house from the authorities in Ballymena. This is redlined for agricultural buildings only, you know?"

"So they might say no?"

"Oh they'll say yes, Mr Macdonald is very well-connected, but it'll take a wee while."

"How long?"

"Six months, or even up to a year to get the planning permission for the house. If they give it for this one they'll have to give it for all of them along this road."

"How long to build it?"

"Four or five months if he turns the whole crew loose on it."

"So when can we think about moving in?"

"Well, if you're lucky the end of the year."

"And if we're unlucky?"

"The autumn of 1989."

"And if we're very unlucky with planning permission and building delays?"

"The spring of 1990?"

Sigh of relief.

I was a conservative animal. I didn't like to move and I liked living on Coronation Road, but 1990 seemed like a very, very long way away. The 1990s were the future. In the 90s things were bound to be very different from now. Thatcher would be gone. Kinnock would be Prime Minister. According to Gerry Anderson's *Space 1999* we would all be living in colonies on the moon at the end of the decade, although that, admittedly, seemed a little bit unlikely.

So why the big fit, Duffy? You're a lucky man. Lucky to be alive. Lucky to have Beth and Emma. So what if you end up out here in the sticks in some bullshit Proddy mansion? Small price to pay isn't it?

"Mr Macdonald's daughter, she's a feisty one, isn't she?" Vaughn said.

"Aye."

"Good-looking."

"Steady, mate. This is the mother of my child."

"You remember that line from the old John Wayne film?"

"I remember it," I said.

"Two women in the house and one of them a redhead," presumably was the quote he was referring to from *The Quiet Man*, although when I thought about my actions of this morning "Life's tough and even tougher when you're stupid," from *The Sands of Iwo Jima*, floated into my mind.

Vaughn nodded and offered me a cigarette. I was still gagging for one but I shook my head.

"Look, can someone give me a lift back to Carrickfergus, please? I've got work to do this morning."

"A lift? That shouldn't be a problem. Troy!"

Yeah, back to Carrick. Interview the victim's wife. Establish the insolubility of this case without eyewitness or forensic evidence. Log it in the yellow file. Hoof it to the flower shop and the chocolate shop and apologise big time: *I overreacted, Beth. Very generous on the part of your da. Might take us two years to move in so we'll stay here just for now . . .*

And maybe in those two years she'll learn to love this part of Carrick? Maybe, Duffy, maybe. As the Russians say, getting what you want sometimes requires moving like the knight in chess: forward and to the left.

5: INSPECTOR DALZIEL

When I arrived at Carrickfergus RUC barracks there was an air of embarrassment hovering over the place. In my experience, Ulster Protestants were capable of being embarrassed by everything and anybody so I wasn't particularly alarmed by this.

I *was* worried when Crabbie and Lawson intercepted me at the top of the stairs.

"Morning, Sean," Crabbie said darkly.

"Oh God, what's amiss? It's not about our Bulgarian, is it? She didn't escape or hang herself or anything like that?"

"No, it's not about her. She's fine. The victim support unit has been with her all morning."

"What's the victim support unit?"

"WPC Green," Lawson said.

"Oh, OK. And the translator?"

"Apparently he's at Carrick Train Station. We've sent a car for him. He should be here in about five minutes," Crabbie explained.

"So what's wrong?"

"Chief Superintendent Strong is here with a couple of people from HR and Dr Havercamp and a nurse," Lawson said.

"Dr Havercamp?"

"It's the fitness tests. The Chief Constable has given an order that this year the RUC fitness tests are to be held on the same day at every station so that people can't bunk off," Crabbie explained.

"Fitness tests? Jesus, you had me concerned there for a second. Don't worry about those, lads. That's only for beat cops. I haven't done a police fitness assessment since I moved here and that was in 1981."

"How do you keep getting out of it?" Lawson asked, amazed.

"Like I said yesterday. Do you ever listen?"

"I do, I—"

"All you do is call in sick."

"The Chief Inspector says if anyone calls in sick today they will be officially failed," Crabbie said.

"Officially failed? I've never heard such rubbish in my life!" I said. "I'm going to go see him. CID shouldn't have to do this. We don't do foot patrols or go round chasing criminals over the rooftops. We're the brains of the outfit around here."

"I don't mind doing a fitness test," Lawson said.

"Yeah, look at you. But what about McCrabban and me?"

"Don't include me, Sean. I'm fine. I've got the farm to keep me fit. Bringing the sheep in from the high bog that'll get your blood pumping and—" Crabbie began, but I put my hand on his shoulder.

"Don't worry, lads, I'll sort this one out. Fitness tests are for ordinary coppers."

The Chief Inspector was in conference with Chief Superintendent Strong, the HR goons, Inspector Dalziel and Dr Havercamp, who was one of the RUC's medical officers. I knew Kevin Havercamp well because he'd repeatedly refused to give me opiates, sick leave and methaqualone on pretty much every occasion on which I'd asked for them over the last few years. He and Strong, however, did give me pleasant enough welcoming smiles, as opposed to Dalziel, who positively grimaced when he saw it was me.

"Ah Duffy, I've been looking for you," CS Strong said in his low, pleasant Glaswegian burr.

"I've been looking for you too, sir. I just want to offer you my hearty congratulations on your promotion, sir. Thoroughly deserved. Assistant Chief Constable. It brings credit to us all, sir."

"Why thank you, Duffy, that's very good of you to say so. It's not quite official yet though, but when all the t's are crossed I'll have a wee celebration at the police club," he said, his close-cropped ginger beard bristling with pleasure.

"I'll buy the first round, sir. We're all very proud to be in your command, sir."

Strong was positively blushing now.

"Now about this fitness test, sir, I—"

"You're not getting out of it, Sean," Strong said quickly. "Out of your entire CID team only Lawson showed up to do the fitness test last year."

"CID *team*? There's only the three of us."

"Well all three of you will be doing the test this morning. Every man in the station and every man in every other station. This is coming direct from the Chief Constable."

"But sir—"

Strong leaned close and lowered his voice to convey a clandestine atmosphere: "An internal civil service report arrives on Mrs Thatcher's desk that says that the RUC is 'the fattest and least fit' police force in the entire British Isles. Not for publication of course but Mrs T sees red. She calls Jack. Jack calls all the divisional officers and he lays down the law to all of us. OK? This is coming from Number 10. You're going to bloody do your run, Duffy, and your bloody push ups and you're not getting out of it."

"OK, sir," I said meekly. "But we have quite a busy morning this morning. We have a crime victim to console and to interrogate. We've got a translator coming from—"

"You better hop to it then, Duffy. Inspector Dalziel here is leading the men out together. You're all going as a group for security reasons. I'll talk to you in a bit about your case if you want."

"Yes, sir."

"Five minutes, Duffy. Have your men meet me in the car park. Don't worry. It's only a little jog to the castle and back," Dalziel said with an incredibly smug look on his face, as if he'd already seen the future too, a future where I give up halfway wheezing . . .

"Five minutes, no problem, see you down there," I said casually.

Back into CID.

"OK, lads, we're not getting out of it, apparently. Yeah I know it's bollocks but what can you do. Is that Bulgarian here yet?"

"He is. I've sent him downstairs to the cells to be with Mrs Deauville," Crabbie said.

"Put both of them in Interview Room #1 and give them tea and biscuits while I try to find some gutties."

I changed into my old PT kit of shorts and a T-shirt and an ancient pair of Adidas gutties I found in my locker. Crabbie followed me downstairs and got changed into a similarly unused kit. I'd never seen him in shorts before.

"My God I need sunglasses to cope with the white glare coming off your legs, mate," I said.

"You can talk, look at you! Skin and bones, seen healthier corpses fished out of the Lagan," he protested, with more defensive sarcasm that he normally mustered of a morning.

But in truth I did look pretty pale and unappetising in the light of day. And in the reverse of what was supposed to happen I had in fact lost weight and muscle definition since cutting down on the smokes. What Beth saw in me I had no idea.

Lawson looked like a young Adonis in his shorts.

"Look at him, Crabbie, he's like a young Adonis in those shorts," I said.

"Adonis would have been naked, sir," Lawson replied.

"Yeah well, I wouldn't try that with Kenny Dalziel. He'll have you up on a charge. Now listen to me Lawson, I expect you to win the race, for the honour of CID," I said.

"It's not a race, sir."

"It is a race and you're going to win. It's going to be like *Chariots of Fire*. Go get your Walkman, get something good on it."

"I did bring it actually. Do you want to listen, sir?" he said playing a dozen toxic bars of Paul Hewson's singing and David Evans's tedious, predictable and barely competent chord progressions.

"What did you think of that, sir?" Lawson said, grinning like he'd just played me Sibelius's lost Eighth Symphony.

"Anodyne, conformist, radio-friendly bollocks, lacking in soul, grace, intelligence or joy," I could have said but didn't. Lawson was a fragile young man and was hurt easily.

"As long as it gets you over the line first," I said.

I led Crabbie and Lawson downstairs to the car park where it was drizzling, cold and grey. Dalziel and the other men were waiting under the overhang. No sign of the Chief Inspector or Chief Superintendent Strong. How'd they get out of it? Some pigs are more equal than others.

"There you are, Duffy!" Dalziel said. "We've been waiting for you."

I took him by the elbow and led him away from the others.

I offered him my hand and he reluctantly shook it. "Kenny, look, if I was out of order yesterday I'm sorry. And I shouldn't have raised my voice. We're all in this together. Us against the enemy you know? And I should have said congratulations on the promotion. OK?"

"Is this you apologising?"

"I'm apologising, yes."

Dalziel's face cracked a little, but then assumed its previous fixity.

"I'm sorry too, Duffy, but I'm still going to make a formal report about you. You can't say stuff like that over the switchboard and around the office. You set a bad example for the other officers. Ill discipline is infectious and without discipline what are we?"

I disengaged my hand from his, muttering "dick".

"What did you say!"

"Nothing. Are we ready to go? There's over twenty men getting soaked here."

"Twenty-six to be exact," Kenny said.

"Or over twenty, to not be exact. Come on, blow your whistle or whatever you do."

"All right! Everybody ready? Let's go!" Kenny said and started the stopwatch.

We had to run a kilometre in under eight minutes which was the distance approximately from the police station to the castle and back.

We set off at a run straight into the teeth of a stiff east wind and sea spray. Although we were going along the seafront and although we were all kitted out primarily in white shorts and T-shirts it did not look remotely like the scene from *Chariots of Fire*. Only half a dozen officers – including Lawson and Dalziel – managed to get back to the station before the eight-minute mark. Every other cop in the barracks failed. I made it in twelve minutes, just behind McCrabban. For the last two hundred metres I thought I was having a heart attack, but at least I made it in running. Some of the fatter sergeants couldn't walk the distance in under twenty minutes.

Soaked, cold and wheezing I hit the showers downstairs.

"Fitness test for CID, never heard of such a thing," I muttered to myself. I dried, changed and I was back upstairs in my office with a restorative vodka gimlet when the Chief Inspector knocked on the door.

"Come in!"

He entered with a clipboard and an air of gloom.

"Ah sir, how were the results?"

He sat down and looked glumly at the stats on the clipboard in front of him. "Everyone failed except for Lawson, Dalziel, Pollock, Hitch, O'Neill and McClusky."

"Can I have a look, sir?"

He handed it over and I was pleased to see that Lawson had indeed come in first.

"This isn't going to look good on the report," he said.

"Just do what all the other stations do," I suggested.

"And what's that, Duffy?" he asked.

"Fake the results. As long as they're on a bell curve and there are a few outliers they'll believe it."

McArthur laughed bitterly. "If only, Sean. But Chief Superintendent Strong is still here and Dalziel timed everyone, too."

McArthur looked distracted and reflective. I didn't know him well but I could tell that there was something else that was bothering him.

"This isn't about the bloody fitness test is it, sir?"

He shook his head. "Can I get a drink?"

"Sorry, sir, don't know where my manners were. Vodka gimlet?"

"What's in it?"

"The way I make it is lime juice, vodka, ice and soda to taste. It's very refreshing."

"I'll take a stiff one."

I poured him a glass. He drank it and nodded appreciatively while I topped mine up.

"Surprisingly tart," he said and put the glass on the table.

"Isn't it?" I said sitting down again.

"Look, Duffy, there's things you need to know."

"What things?"

He smiled. "I'm on my way out."

"Resigning? At your age, surely you—"

"Promotion. I'm probably moving up to divisional level in the summer. Strong's promotion to Assistant Chief Constable creates a vacancy."

"I see."

"Victor McClusky will be made the new Chief Super and I'll get his old job."

"Congratulations, sir. Superintendent. You deserve it."

"No, they're not making me Superintendent just yet but I assume that will come with the new responsibilities."

"Still, congratulations. Divisional level."

His jaw clenched. "I'm not a complete fool, Duffy, I know what you're thinking. *Here am I languishing at the rank of Inspector for the last five years . . .*"

"Promotion isn't the be all and the—" I tried but McArthur was a salesman who couldn't leave your door until he'd finished his spiel: "I know what you all think in CID. Sean Duffy collars the villains and Chief Inspector McArthur takes the credit if there is any credit."

"That's not what we think at all, sir!"

"Well, it won't be me for much longer. I'll be gone. And I'm sorry to say that I've been told that they are not going to promote you into my place even though you have effective seniority. They will never promote you, Sean. You know that, don't you? I've seen your confidential HR file. It actually says that on it. 'Not to be given additional responsibility'."

"I was told that by someone else who'd seen it."

"Red lines all over it. You have some powerful enemies and I suppose some powerful friends too for them not to have tried to boot you out before now."

McArthur wasn't to know that all my powerful friends had been killed in a helicopter crash on the Mull of Kintyre two years earlier. Now I only had powerful enemies.

"Oh they've tried to boot me out, sir, but I keep hanging on.

So who's getting your job? New broom?"

"Nope. That's why I made you apologise. Dalziel will be made Chief Inspector and he'll be running the show from August onwards. You're going to have to learn to work under him, OK?"

"Kenny Dalziel is being promoted to Chief Inspector a few months after being promoted to Inspector?"

"Yes."

"And he is going to be put in charge of the whole station?"

"Yes." ·

"With all due respect, sir, he's got no talent for command."

"That's the kind of talk I don't want to hear, Sean. I don't want any more comments like that from you or anyone who works for you. OK?"

"Yes, sir."

McArthur shook his head. "I share some of your reservations. I saw his wife once with a bruise on her cheek."

"The fucking bastard."

"I know . . . Look, he's going away this week for his annual leave to Eastbourne and when he comes back I expect relations between you and him to be completely different. Certainly they will need to be fixed by the summer or your life here is going to be untenable."

I said nothing. The rain was lashing the window behind the Chief Inspector's head and in the stormy lough beyond boats were struggling to make headway up the deep water channel to the port of Belfast. This was all some kind of metaphor for my own life.

"Maybe Dalziel will fail the promotion board. Surely they'll see that he's an eejit."

"I wouldn't get your hopes up. He's been practising for the promotion board for years. He's the sort of pencil pushing, risk-adverse type who'll slowly go up the ranks until he's Chief Constable."

I nodded sadly and finished my vodka gimlet.

The Chief Inspector stood up. "You'll remember what I said. No more smart-alec remarks. Make nice. OK? And remember this is just between us."

"Yes, sir," I said, feeling thoroughly beaten now.

"Oh and report to the doctor downstairs. He'll go through your blood work with you and take your pulse. You know the drill."

"Do I have to do that now? I have a witness to interrogate."

"It'll only take five minutes, Sean," he said.

I nodded and when he was gone put on a fresh shirt and tie to look respectable for the doctor.

The phone rang in my office. Switchboard said it was a reporter but I didn't have the time to talk to reporters. "Shall I say you're too busy?" Eileen asked.

"Yeah, that'll do," I said absently. Reporters, of course, hated to be told that you were too busy to speak to them.

Of course the doc's visit did not take five minutes. Not even close. I'd been avoiding Kevin Havercamp for some time, now the bugger was going to get his money's worth.

A sallow-faced, balding, heavy lidded, Uriah Heep of a man, Kevin could take the wind from the sails of even the breeziest of chaps and he caught me when I was already vulnerable.

He made me strip to my boxers and vest. He weighed me, listened to my lungs and took my blood pressure. He stuck me in a dangerous-looking X-ray machine that seem to have been trundled out of 1955 and a grim-faced nurse took a photograph of my internals.

"What's the verdict, doc?" I asked as I put my clothes back on.

"You're 10 stone nothing and your blood pressure is 150 over 95. Are you on hunger strike or something?"

"No."

"So you're just living on cigarettes and whisky now, eh Sean?"

"No. I've cut down on both, actually."

"Well, we'll talk about that in a minute. Have you had trouble breathing lately?"

"Uh, funny you should say that, sometimes in the mornings . . ."

"How were you on the 1K run?"

"CID acquitted itself well. DC Lawson won."

"I wasn't talking about your department, I was talking about you, Sean."

"If I'm honest the last bit of the run was something of a trial."

"Do you ever have any of these symptoms: Shortness of breath? Chest tightness or pain? Trouble sleeping caused by shortness of breath, coughing or wheezing? A whistling or wheezing sound when exhaling?"

"Sometimes shortness of breath."

"Do you have coughing or wheezing attacks that are worsened by a respiratory virus, such as a cold or the flu?"

"Now and again, yeah."

"Do your breathing difficulties worsen when you are exposed to airborne allergens, such as pollen, animal dander, mould, cockroaches and dust mites?"

"Maybe."

"Or when it's cold air, or like this morning when there's physical activity?"

"What have I got? Is it cancer?"

"There's no evidence of cancer on your X-ray or in your blood work."

"Well, that's a relief. Just a cold then, is it?"

"You've got asthma, Sean."

"Asthma? Are you sure? I never had that as a kid."

"Well you've got it now. We've caught it early and for that you're lucky. I'll give you a leaflet explaining how your condition manifested itself and explaining the treatment options. I won't go into detail now because I've got a lot to talk to you about and time is pressing."

"Can it be treated?"

"Yes. I'm going to prescribe two different types of inhalers for you. The first is an inhaled bronchial steroid that you will take every morning. It will help prevent asthma attacks by reducing swelling and mucus production in the airways. As a result, the airways will be less sensitive and less likely to react to asthma triggers and cause asthma symptoms. I'll also prescribe a bronchodilator which will relieve the symptoms of asthma by relaxing the muscles that can tighten around the airways. Short-acting bronchodilator inhalers are often referred to as rescue inhalers and are used to quickly relieve the shortness of breath caused by asthma."

"OK. What else did you—"

"Can we talk about the cigarettes?" he said with a black look I didn't like at all.

"There's no need for that face, Kevin. It's totally ironic, I haven't had a cigarette all day. I've been cutting down for months. I have cut down from two packs a day to half a pack. Do I get any credit for that?"

"The ironic thing about that is the fact that you expect credit for only smoking ten cigarettes a day."

I nodded. "All right, so what else am I doing wrong?"

"Can we talk about the drink, Sean?"

"What about it?"

"How many units of alcohol would you say that you drink a week?"

"I don't know. Twenty?"

"Do you know what a unit it is?"

"Yeah. A beer, a glass of whisky, a glass of wine all equal one unit."

"How many units of beer do you drink a week?"

"Just beer? A couple of pints at lunchtime. One, maybe two, after work with the lads. I'm not a big beer drinker to be honest, not like some blokes around here. At the end of day I'll usually just have a whisky or a quiet vodka gimlet and go to bed," I said to him, not unpacking the fact that this was a vodka gimlet in a pint glass.

He looked pained.

"A pint of beer is two units. Just in beer alone you're drinking eight units of beer a day. That's fifty-six units a week, just in beer. That's twice the recommended dose for someone your age. And if you add in the vodka gimlets and the whiskies . . . You need to cut down, Sean."

"It's not just me. It's everyone in this station."

"Yes I know. And I've been telling everyone in this station. You all need to cut down on your alcohol consumption."

"How much do you drink?"

"I don't drink. I'm a Free Presbyterian."

"I bet I outlive you."

Kevin sighed and shook his head. "If I was a betting man I'd bet that you won't actually, Sean. But listen there's something else. Something more serious."

"Go on . . ."

"On your blood work you tested positive for cannabis."

I nodded.

"And in the past you've asked me for dihydrocodeine and morphine on a number of occasions."

"For me back! Jesus! I was in a Land Rover that looped the loop and I've been shot once and blown up twice."

"Opiates for pain relief and the cannabis for what?"

"We're off the record here? This is a doctor–patient thing?"

"Of course."

"Now and again just to relax."

"I'm not going to report this to any higher authority but I can't sign you as fit for duty while you're smoking dope, Sean."

"That seems a bit extreme, Kev. You know I'm the only one that does any work around here."

"I'll give you a month, Sean. You'll report to me for another blood test. If I don't see an improvement in your tox levels I'm going to put you on restricted duty. It's for your own good, you know. You have a wife and child now, I believe."

"Girlfriend and child."

"You need to change your act, Sean. Alcohol consumption down to under twenty units a week. If you can't quit try and get your cigarette smoking down to two or three a day and you will stop smoking marijuana immediately. If I see it showing up in your blood work again, I'll have you on restricted duty permanently. I can't have stoned coppers on the job, even detectives as capable as yourself. You should know better."

"It's stressful out there, doc," I said wondering what Kev would have said if he'd tested me in 1985 when at one point during the Anglo-Irish Agreement crisis I'd been taking cocaine, hash, ciggies, moonshine, Valium and diamorphine pills – usually before lunch.

"I know it is and I'm not expecting you or any of your colleagues to be Supermen, but if you want to remain on active duty you'll do what I tell you."

"Christ, this has been a miserable day so far," I muttered to myself.

"See it as a wake-up call. Here's the prescriptions for your asthma inhalers," he said, handing me a couple of scripts.

"If you put me on restricted duty, who is going to run Carrick CID?"

"Sergeant McCrabban will have to do it."

"McCrabban? He smokes a pipe. I don't see you telling him off."

"I've told him off already. Now act your age, Sean, and buck up your ideas."

I took the prescriptions and left the makeshift examination room with my tail between my legs. I clearly wasn't the only one who had gotten bad news from the doc and there was a foul atmosphere in the air. I was still punchy and pissed off when I finally went upstairs to interview Mrs Deauville with the help of the Bulgarian translator. This was where the day began to right itself and where I began to be lulled into a false sense of security. *I could fix things with Beth. My health was going to get better. Maybe Dalziel would shoot himself in the foot either metaphorically or literally before the summer* . . . And anyway there was a job to do. Interviewing a witness/suspect in a murder inquiry was a hell of a way to clear out the cobwebs. Question and answer, question and answer, building a picture, brick by smoky brick. Carving important data points and timelines out of an information blizzard, law out of chaos, order out of entropy.

Yeah, right.

6: MR DEAUVILLE'S INTERESTING PAST

The Bulgarian translator was in fact much more than a mere translator. He was actually a mid-ranking consular official called Pytor Yavarov who had been based in Dublin for nearly two years. A slight, handsome man with an old-fashioned Clark Gable moustache he had dressed himself in what he perhaps thought was the style of an old-fashioned Irish country gentlemen: tweeds, white linen shirt, brown Oxfords, with a rather attractive paisley blue tie. He was pale of face, blue of eye, with a shock of curly black hair. On perhaps any other person in Carrickfergus such a look would have drawn forth sniggers but Yavarov was sitting there with such poise and quiet assertiveness that somehow he managed to pull the whole thing off. Mrs Deauville was a different kettle of fish. Chubby, twenty-something, with dark rings round her eyes she was dressed entirely in sweats: Adidas trackie bottoms, Nike hoodie top. Her hair was a short bowl-cut dyed peroxide blonde. She was wearing a single flip flop that she flipped on and off the stubby crimson-painted toes of her left foot. Like I say, she wasn't unattractive and if she'd stayed away from the tanning shop and let her natural brown hair grow out you would have said that she was a looker. They made an odd couple sitting there in Interview Room #1 muttering together in Bulgarian, waiting for us to show up. Neither of them looked Bulgarian, whatever Bulgarians were supposed to look like.

We were watching them through the big two-way mirror that ran along one of the walls of the incident room.

"Mrs Deauville seems to have calmed down a good bit," I said.

"Well, she hasn't tried to stab WPC Warren or the man from the embassy," Crabbie said.

"Did either of you get a chance to read the reports from their neighbours?"

"I read them this morning," Lawson said.

"Fights? Screaming? Yelling? Anything like that?"

"No one heard any arguments or any disputes or anything like that. And no one saw anything on the night of the murder," Lawson said, handing me the interviews with the Deauville neighbours. These canvassing statements were practically worthless. For all we knew, Mr and Mrs Deauville might have been fighting like cats and dogs every single night since they moved in but no one in Sunnylands would ever tell us that. A drug dealer was bad, a woman who murders her husband was bad, but an informer was a more terrible creature by far than either.

"I also saw you over at the fax machine, Lawson."

"More detailed autopsy results came through."

"Anything interesting in them?" I asked Lawson.

"Death by crossbow bolt in the stomach, which we knew. But the preliminary toxicology results were quite interesting."

"How so?"

"He was clean as a whistle. He was a dealer but not a user."

"Didn't smoke the profits. Smart guy. Oh I should tell you both that Carrick's paramilitaries are not going to be claiming this one. Neither the UVF nor the UDA say they did it. My informant tells me that although Mr Deauville was an independent contractor he dutifully paid his protection money."

"But he actually didn't get any protection," Crabbie said.

"No."

"Who was this informant?" Crabbie asked.

"Andy Young."

"Well, he would know."

"Yeah he would."

"So if the UVF and UDA didn't kill him who did?" Lawson asked.

"Young could have been lying to me. There's no honour among thieves and even less among drug dealers and paramilitaries," I said.

"I just can't see anyone else driving into the heart of UVF territory to execute some random drug dealer," Crabbie said.

"There's been no statement at all so far from this Direct Action Against Drug Dealers group, which there probably would have been by now if they'd been involved," I said.

"So that leaves Mrs Deauville," Lawson said.

Crabbie shook his head. "I don't think Mrs Deauville did it either."

"Why? We haven't even talked to her yet. And she is violent, as you can testify," I said.

"Remember that other drug dealer I was telling you about who was shot on Tuesday but survived?"

"Yeah."

"Well, forensic confirms that all three crossbow bolts came from the same weapon," Crabbie said definitively.

"How did they know that?"

"The way they know things."

"You talked to someone over there?"

"Yeah. Jimmy Nichol."

"When was this?"

"When you were in with the doctor."

"What else did he tell you?"

"Apart from the victim's blood there was no DNA on the crossbow bolts."

"And all three bolts came from the same crossbow?"

"Yup."

"Where is that other victim? Morrison something, right?"

"Ivan Morrison. He's still in Larne Hospital. Lawson and I got a full statement out of him on Tuesday night."

"And he doesn't know who shot him?"

"He's not talking. Says he didn't see or hear anything. They shot him from behind and drove off in a car."

"Well, I'd like to talk to him," I said.

"Better do it soon, Sean. If some bloke shot me in the back and was going around shooting other drug dealers I'd be on the boat to England pretty sharpish."

"Good call. We'll go see him today. But I don't see how you think that the attack on Morrison rules out Mrs Deauville. How do you know she didn't shoot Mr Morrison first on Tuesday to establish a pattern and then shoot her husband on Wednesday?"

Crabbie conceded the point. "If that's true it'll be a murder charge then," he said.

Lawson seemed puzzled by this statement of the bleeding obvious. "We know it's murder," he said.

"If it was a crime of passion, we could have charged her with manslaughter, but if she really did shoot Morrison too then it establishes a mens rea and we have no choice but to take a murder rap to the DPP."

Lawson nodded. "Oh I see. So by being too clever by half to throw us off the scent she's got herself done for murder."

"I still don't think she did it," Crabbie insisted.

I looked at him squarely in the face. He had good instincts, McCrabban. He smiled at me and started his filling his pipe.

"Oi, didn't you get a lecture from Dr Havercamp about smoking?"

"He said I was as fit as a fiddle," Crabbie said.

"Did he? He said I was a mess."

"You should switch to a pipe."

"He told me to cut out tobacco completely."

"Aye. Well, he has a point, King James was against tobacco and he translated the Bible," Crabbie said.

"A hundred years from now we're going to discover that tobacco is good for us."

"No we won't," Lawson said.

"Anybody find Deauville's criminal record?" I asked.

"Yes, I looked that out for you and put it on your desk," Crabbie said.

"Run and get it, will you, Lawson?"

When Lawson was out of the room I told Crabbie about Dalziel's coming apotheosis.

McCrabban nodded dourly. "I could see it in the cards as soon as they promoted Strong to ASC. Strong to ASC, McClusky into Strong's place and McArthur into McClusky's job. That would leave a gap here and although you're the senior officer they can't promote you because you've ruffled too many feathers. They can't promote me because I have no administrative experience and I'm only a detective sergeant so it has to be Dalziel. They can't bump him from Sergeant to Chief Inspector so they make him an Inspector for now and Chief Inspector in August when McArthur leaves."

"That's a fine bit of detective work. Why didn't you tell me?"

"I didn't want to spoil your holiday. I know it's not very Christian for me to say but I don't particularly like Kenny—"

Lawson came back in with Deauville's file and we killed our mutinous conversation.

The file contained a few surprises:

Born Belfast 1945. He had gone to the relatively posh Methodist College and then to Queens University where he had briefly read English before being rusticated for being drunk and disorderly. Unemployed for a bit and, in that most turbulent of years, 1968, he had joined the police as a "special constable" but had resigned in early 1969, presumably having had his fill of beating up peaceful Catholic Civil Rights marchers. He had evidently moved to England after that, because in 1975 he was arrested for an armed robbery of a Brixton post office. The jury of his peers acquitted him of that offence but in 1978 he was convicted of insurance fraud in a case of an Irish pub that had burned to the ground. He served eighteen months in a minimum security institution and then apparently moved north. In 1980 he was arrested for assaulting a man in a bar in Bradford but the charges were dropped. In 1982 he assaulted another man in Manchester and again the charges were dropped. In 1984 he was arrested for another armed robbery on a post office and this time he got three years.

I handed the file back to Lawson. "Not a very successful criminal. But he wasn't a complete idiot. He went to Queens. All the best people go to Queens."

"Is that where you went, sir?" Lawson asked innocently.

"It is indeed."

"He had quite a varied criminal record though, didn't he? Bank robbery, insurance fraud," Crabbie said.

"Aye he's tried a few things," I agreed. "But no drug dealing. Drug dealing is a new arrow in his quiver, if you'll excuse the association."

"He's done everything except for getting a real job," Crabbie said.

"And he was a former policeman, did you see that, sir?" Lawson said.

"Well an 'Ulster Special Constable'. You can't really call him a policeman," Crabbie said, quick to defend the honour of the RUC.

"Is that like a reservist?" Lawson asked.

"No, not the same thing at all. When were you born, son?" I asked.

"1967."

"You've never heard of the B Specials?" Crabbie said.

Lawson shook his head. "I've heard of them but I don't really know what they are."

"In 1922 the Ulster Special Constabulary was set up to support the police. There were the A Specials – full timers, B Specials – part-timers and C Specials – volunteers who didn't get paid. The A Specials were absorbed into the RUC and became regular policemen. The C Specials were disbanded and that left the B Specials," I explained.

"Back in 1968 in Belfast they thought there was going to be an all-out war between the Protestants and the Catholics. The police were ridiculously undermanned so they hired hundreds of B Special constables to fill the gaps. Some of them were decent enough but there was a pretty high percentage of thugs who joined just looking for some action," Crabbie said.

"They were poorly trained, poorly equipped and the vetting wasn't all it could have been," I added.

"The B Specials performed so badly in the first two years of the Troubles that at the end of 1969 they were disbanded completely," Crabbie said.

"But maybe his police training helped him in his criminal career?" Lawson suggested.

"It doesn't look like that criminal career was too successful either, was it?"

"We don't know that. The criminal record only shows the crimes he was done for," Lawson said.

I nodded, yawned and stood up. "Good point. All right then lads, enough procrastination, let's talk to the widow Deauville."

We were about to knock on the door of Interview Room #1 when Kenny Dalziel shimmered out of nowhere and intercepted us.

"Ah, Duffy, I wanted to talk to you about a couple of things before I leave."

"Can't do it, Kenny, got to interview a witness in a murder investigation. Police work, if you know what that is."

Kenny grimaced and I could see the gears working behind those vinegary black eyes, *patience Kenny he'll pay for this, just a couple of months now and he'll pay . . .*

"You and Sergeant McCrabban both failed the run. You'll have to take it again in a month and pass it if you want to be considered fit for duty. When I get back from my holidays I'll be conducting a PT class every morning. Attendance is mandatory."

"No, I'm afraid we can't do that, Kenny. We're too busy in CID. Small department. Lot of cases. Dr Havercamp already has McCrabban and me on a fitness regime. Was that all?"

Kenny's lips pursed. "No, it's not all. I've been told that one of your witnesses is Bulgarian, is that right?"

"That's correct."

"Last year you and Constable Lawson went to Finland to supposedly follow up on a lead. That little trip cost the station a thousand pounds. And you've also been to England and Scotland on the station's shilling."

"So?"

"No trips to Bulgaria, Duffy. We can't afford to pay for all your gallivanting around. No trips to Bulgaria, no trips to the South of France, no trips anywhere, just stay within your budget. This is a case of a dead drug dealer in Carrick. If I was a detective I could close one like that in a couple of days."

"But you're not a detective, are you?"

Kenny's eyes again boring into me. I took him to the end of the corridor. "I hear you're going to Eastbourne?" I said.

"I'm paying for that. It's my holiday."

"That's not what I'm driving at. I was just thinking that's where they have Beachy Head, isn't it?"

"Yes."

"Well, don't be tempted to jump off, Kenny. I appreciate that it must be a fucking nightmare to wake up every morning and realise that you are still you, but suicide is not the answer, old cock."

It was a mild jibe, well within the bounds allowed in two officers of equal rank, but Kenny reacted as if I'd asked him to drink a pint of Margaret Thatcher's piss at the Cenotaph on Poppy Day.

"I've had enough of your insolence, Duffy. You should have been out long ago if you weren't a fucking fe . . ." he began, but his voice died in his throat before he could completely sabotage himself.

"A what?"

"A nothing."

"A 'fucking fenian', is that what you were going to say?"

"I never said that!"

"Yeah, well it's the thought that counts, isn't it? Now if you don't mind, some of us have bloody work to do around here," I said, pushing past him, marching down the corridor, knocking on the interview room door and going inside without waiting for a reply.

It was another exit Bette Davis or Rosalind Russell or even Joan Crawford would have been proud of.

7: THE BULGARIANS AND THE BEL TEL

Introductions were made and I sat opposite the Bulgarians with Lawson and McCrabban. WPC Warren excused herself and I gave her a nod of thanks for holding the fort for the entire morning.

I lit my first cigarette of the day and it tasted fantastic. Calmed me the fuck right down.

"Mrs Deauville, I am so sorry for your loss," I said and Yavarov translated for me.

A long stream of Bulgarian followed that Mr Yavarov did not translate.

"What did she say?"

"You are in charge of this investigation?" Yavarov asked in perfect and only slightly accented English.

"Yes, I am in charge," I said

"Mrs Deauville says she spent the night in police cells," Yavarov said, bristling.

"That's right."

"Was she charged with a crime?" Yavarov asked.

"No, but she could have been."

"Was she a suspect in her husband's death?"

"We can't rule anyone out at this stage."

"Her husband was murdered and you put her in the cells. I will protest this to my embassy!"

"No, you won't. You won't kick up any kind of fuss at all. Mrs

Deauville stabbed one of my officers in front of a dozen witnesses. My man has decided not to press charges, but that could
change if we don't have Mrs Deauville's complete cooperation.
Assaulting a police officer is a very serious offence indeed," I
said.

Yavarov was clearly impressed by this (perhaps intimidating
the public was how things were done back home) and a brief,
furious discussion followed in Bulgarian with Mrs D.

"She will tell you everything she knows," he said at the end
of it.

"Let's start with the timeline," I said to Yavarov.

"What do you want to know?" Mrs Deauville asked.

"You speak English?" Yavarov, Crabbie and I asked together.

"Of course! I am travel agent. I speak English, Turkish,
German," she said.

"Why didn't you speak English before now?" I asked.

She gave us a sly knowing glance. "I not say anything without
my lawyer," she muttered triumphantly.

"He's not a lawyer. You're not a lawyer, are you?"

Yavarov shook his head.

"He protect me from police tricks. Frank always talk about
police tricks. Police they arrest you, put drugs in your pocket,
make up lies. You will not do this now!"

"We don't do things like that in Carrick CID," I said.

"All police, all same, everywhere!" Mrs Deauville said.

I sighed. "The night your husband was murdered, where
were you between the hours of midnight and two in the morning, Mrs Deauville?"

"You call me Elena. Please. No one call me Mrs Deauville,"
she said.

"Where were you last night between the hours of midnight
and two in the morning, Elena?"

"Frank go out drinking Rangers Club. No women allowed
Rangers Club so I no go. I know he come back late so I make

chips and leave in pan and go to bed."

"What time did you go to bed?"

"Eleven, a little before, perhaps."

"Where is your bedroom in the house? Front or back?"

"Big back bedroom."

"And did you hear anything during the night?"

"No, I sleep until morning."

"So you have no alibi between the hours of midnight and two am?"

"I sleep."

"And what happened after you woke up?"

"I look for Frank. He not in bed or downstairs on sofa. I hear crowd outside. I open front door—" she dissolved into sobs that shook her whole body. If she was indeed a murderess she was also a pretty good actress.

I gave her a tissue and let her compose herself.

"And then what happened?"

"I hug Frank and then I call ambulance and police and then this one (she pointed at McCrabban) tells me I cannot touch my husband. I must go inside and let policemen make jokes and take photographs while Frank lies dead on ground!"

I looked at Crabbie.

"I assure you, Sean, no one was making jokes. You know I don't allow that sort of thing," Crabbie said defensively.

"So you didn't see who killed Mr Deauville?"

"I no see."

"Do you have any idea who would want Mr Deauville dead?"

"No. Frank well liked. Make many good friends."

"How did you meet Mr Deauville?"

"We meet in Villa Armira."

"You'll have to elaborate on that a bit."

She cocked her head at the word elaborate.

Yavarov explained what I was after.

"Villa Armira, Ivaylovgrad, two years ago. I am tour guide

to Roman ruins. Frank is very charming man. Very funny. We become friends. We go out. He come back for another holiday few months later. We write to one another. He come back again and this time he propose to me. We get married and we ask to move to UK. Permission granted."

"It says in our file that Francis Deauville was forty-three, you're what, twenty-five? Bit of an age gap, no?"

Crabbie shot me a *you-can-talk-Sean* look from under his eyebrows.

"Age is of no matter when people in love," Elena said dismissively.

"Very true, Mrs Deauville, very true. Now, maybe I'm wrong but I thought it was quite difficult to move from an Eastern European country to the west?"

Elena scoffed. "Nothing difficult if you have money."

"And Mr Deauville had money?"

"Frank talk to officials, get permits. No problem."

"And you got married where?"

"In London. Frank's mother come for wedding. Frank has mother in home in Frinton-on-Sea. You know Frinton-on-Sea?"

"No. I'm afraid not."

"You didn't want to live there, in England?" Crabbie asked.

"Frank have house in Bangor that he inherit from uncle. I come see, I like. It remind me of Black Sea."

"I've never heard that comparison before. House in Bangor, eh? The address?"

"4 Cold Harbour Road. Nothing there now. House burn in fire."

"A fire?"

"House burn in fire, we have insurance claim in."

I gave Lawson a look. "Go check out this fire for me, will ya?" He nodded and went off.

"So, Mrs Deauville, did Mr Deauville have any enemies?"

"Frank have no enemies. Frank makes friends everywhere he go, no enemies."

"Didn't the North Down UVF tell him to leave Bangor last year or they would kill him? Was that what the fire was all about?"

"Frank asked to leave. He leave. No hassle. We move to Carrickfergus, we make friends here. No hassle. Frank very cooperative man. Make friends everywhere. Two months in Carrick no problems. Fire happen after we leave. Whole house burn. We have insurance claim in."

"What did Mr Deauville do for a living here?"

"Like I say, he unemployed."

"Where did he get the money to pay off all these Eastern European officials?"

"He have inheritance. I tell you. Uncle who die."

"We can check that."

"Check it. Uncle die, maybe Auntie die. I give you solicitor name."

"We'll take those details from you later. How much was this inheritance?"

"I not sure."

"Look, let's not beat about the bush, Frank was a drug dealer, wasn't he?" I asked.

"He unemployed," Elena insisted.

"You never saw him with any drugs?"

"No drugs. He unemployed."

"So you had no trouble after you moved to Carrick?"

"No trouble."

"He paid the protection money in Carrick?"

"I do not know this 'protection money'. But we have no trouble before we move or after we move."

Lawson came back in with details of the fire in Bangor. Arson, but whether by the Deauvilles or the Bangor paramilitaries it was impossible to say. Insurance investigators could sort that one out.

"How many times have you been back to Bulgaria since you got married?" I asked.

Elena shrugged.

"It's very easy to check with the passport authorities."

"I go back maybe six times to see my mother and father."

"You've been back to Bulgaria six times in the last year!"

"Maybe seven. Eight? Who knows?"

"What were you doing on all these trips to Bulgaria?"

"I visit my mother and father and sisters in Sofia."

"And did you bring anything back on these trips from Bulgaria?"

She looked puzzled. "What you mean? I bring Bulgar vodka. Is good. Legal to bring three litres."

"Did you ever bring back anything gaffer-taped to your body?"

"What you mean?"

"A kilo of brown tar heroin perhaps?"

She looked affronted. "You say I drug smuggler?"

"I must object to this line of questioning, Inspector Duffy!" Yavarov said. "This lady's husband was murdered!"

"Look, I don't give a crap if you smuggled in drugs or not, I'm investigating a homicide and there's no way I can find out who killed your husband unless you give me all the details of your husband's affairs," I attempted.

She lit a cigarette and leaned back in her chair. A hardness descended over her face that I recognised from years of these interrogations. She was clearly broken up over her husband's death but come hell or high water she wasn't going to tell me anything about Frank's narcotics business lest she herself be implicated.

"I give you my word that this will just be between us," I said.

She laughed bitterly. "What value word of policeman!"

"Elena, please, you don't seem to understand how the RUC works. I'm not the drug squad, I don't care what you've done or what Frank did. I just want to catch the man who did this."

"Frank unemployed."

There followed ten more minutes of this as first I and then

McCrabban and finally Lawson attempted to get her to admit that either her husband was a drug dealer or that he had made any enemies in four decades of walking planet Earth. Elena was having none of it. There had been no bricks through windows, no threatening phone calls, no strangers accosting them on the street, no punishment beatings or threatened punishment beatings. Frank was unemployed, he didn't associate with criminals, all the trips back to Bulgaria had merely been to visit her parents and sisters.

"Mrs Deauville, Elena, look, it's in your interest to help us."

"What you do now? Say you contact immigration authority and find out if my visa in order? Threaten me? Well Frank sort everything out. My visa in order!" she said, flicking ash aggressively into the ashtray in front of her.

I tried another tack. "Was everything OK between you and Mr Deauville? Any marital difficulties?"

She smiled and said something in Bulgarian to Yavarov. Addressing Lawson she said: "Now your boss try this: blame me for Frank's death. Say I do it and unless cooperate get murder charge. Your boss good man. Yes, yes."

"Well, you don't have an alibi, do you?"

"No. I sleep."

"Ever fire a crossbow, Elena?"

"I never fire crossbow. I never see crossbow. Be good policeman, search house for crossbow."

"We already searched your house for a crossbow and didn't find one, but that doesn't mean anything. You could have walked it to the end of the Fisherman's Quay and thrown it in the sea."

"Go to crossbow shop, show crossbow shop man my photograph, ask if I buy crossbow."

I gave Crabbie a little nod and he nodded back. "And if the crossbow shop man doesn't remember you or you bought it at a second-hand shop does that mean you're off the hook?" Crabbie said.

"Why I kill Frank?"

"Why do husbands kill wives and wives kill husbands?" I said.

Her violet eyes flashed. "Frank and I very happy. He lucky to have me. I lucky to have him. Why I kill him? I love him," she said and her eyes teared up.

She didn't mean to lose it but the tears became the full water-works and all of us in the interview room were quite affected.

The policeman, like the doctor and the paramedic, treads a fine line between distance and humanity. Get too close to a victim or a suspect or a patient and you can lose yourself in the darkness of their case; but remain too distant from the suffering and the pain and you become a robot, a machine, a chilly socio-path. Like old Inspector Laidlaw across the sheugh you found yourself in the dilemma of either indulging in grief by proxy or imitating a stone.

No stone me.

I leaned across that big old oak table of Interview Room #1 and took her hand in mine and squeezed.

"We'll do our best to find your husband's killer, Elena. We want to help, we really do," I said.

She nodded and the tears flowed and the hurt on her face could not possibly be fake. You can't fake grief like that.

"You can't fake grief like that," I said to Crabbie at the coffee machine.

"Nope. I don't think you can," he said.

"You and Lawson keep at her. I have to pop home for half an hour to deal with a small family emergency, OK?"

"Is the baby all right?" Crabbie asked, aghast.

"The baby's fine, mate. Just a wee issue with moving house, you know?"

"You're moving house?"

"Maybe. I don't know."

"After we get her formal statement do we let Mrs Deauville go?" Crabbie asked.

"I don't think we can really let her go just yet, can we? She's obviously been smuggling heroin from Bulgaria every month for the last year. How else does Frank the bank robber suddenly become Frank the pusher?"

Crabbie winced. "The poor woman's devastated and as you yourself said that's not quite in our purview is it, Sean?"

"We need her cooperation and if we can use leverage to get it that's what we'll do," I said sternly.

Crabbie game me a dour look of disapproval and shook his head. I could see his point but I wanted to find that lock-up and get all we could from Mrs D.

"And get Lawson to get the local constabulary to notify the mother in Frinton-on-Sea. See if they can dig up any dirt."

"All right," Crabbie said.

"Look, no need for the long face. I'll be back in half an hour. We'll finish up with Mrs Deauville and if we're satisfied that we've gotten all we can we'll send her home. We still have this Morrison fella, the first victim, to interview before he legs it."

Outside to the Beemer in the chilly early March rain but the dark blue 1988 model 535i Sport was not waiting there like an expectant panther.

"Where's me bloody car . . . oh yeah. Shit."

Back inside the cop shop where I asked Sergeant Prentice to sign out a Land Rover for me.

A three-ton police Land Rover chugging along the Scotch Quarter, over the Horseshoe Bridge and then up the Barn Road and Coronation Road.

#113 Coronation Road where my Beemer *was* waiting for me. Park the Rover. Up the path. In through the front door.

Silence.

"Hello?"

Silence.

The fuck?

Kitchen table. A note: "Don't be alarmed, Sean. I've taken

Emma to stay with my folks for a while. You can phone me there but please don't phone me today. I know what you're like."

I crumpled up the note, grabbed the telephone and dialled the number.

"Hello?" Beth said.

"It's me."

"I knew you'd call. And I knew it would be at lunchtime. How'd your fitness thing go? Did you get out of it?"

"What's going on, Beth?"

"I think we need a little break from each other, Sean. Clearly."

"Look, I was way out of line this morning. I know that now. You want to move house? That's fine with me. You know I'm not a morning person. It was all just a bit much. I'm sorry."

A long pause.

Crying.

"I'm so glad to hear you say that, Sean. Really, I am."

"You forgive me? I know it's no excuse but I'm under a lot of stress."

Another long pause. "I forgive you, Sean. But you can't act like that in front of Emma. She's just a little girl."

"What are you doing now? I'll come down there and get you."

"No, Sean. I'm staying here for a couple of days. It's good for Emma and it's good for me."

"So when are you coming back?"

"Just give me a couple of days, OK?"

"The weekend? Sunday night?"

"Please, Sean, no pressure."

I put my hand over the receiver. "You don't know anything about fucking pressure, sister," I whispered to myself.

I took my hand off the mouthpiece. "OK, sweetie. Give me a call. Have a nice time with your folks and say hi from me . . . You didn't tell them we had a row?"

"Uhm, not as such."

"Good. OK. Give me a call. Love you. Bye."

"OK, Sean, bye."

Asymmetrical response. No "love you too". Fuck.

Back out to the Land Rover in the rain. Check underneath for mercury tilt switch bombs.

None.

Back to the station.

Crabbie meeting me in the incident room.

"Everything OK on the home front?"

"Fine. Any developments on the case?"

"Not really."

"Deauville's mother?"

"Local boys gave her the notification. She's very upset obviously."

"I imagine. Anything helpful from the local plod?"

"She says she doesn't know who killed Mr Deauville and has no knowledge of any drug dealing."

We went back to Interview Room #1 and tried another couple of lines of attack on Mrs Deauville but she wasn't giving us anything. She claimed she didn't know about any off site lock-up or garage. She denied being a drug mule. She said she didn't kill her husband and didn't know who did. The first two statements were obviously lies but all three of us believed the third.

"Did anyone threaten your husband recently?"

"No."

"Did anyone threaten you?"

"No."

"Have there been any problems with the neighbours?"

"No."

"Any anonymous letters or bricks through windows, anything like that?"

"No."

"Anyone following you, or strangers watching the house?"

A tiny hesitation before: "No."

"Are you sure no one's been following you?"

"No. Nobody follow."

"No strangers around the house?"

"No strangers."

"Are you sure?"

"Quite sure. Very sure. Everything normal and then Frank is murdered. Who did this? Who killed Frank?"

"We'll endeavour to find out, Elena."

Pause.

Reverse the shot.

Go close on her face. She's not telling you everything but she's almost certainly not the killer. Eyes – read the eyes for that kind of information.

"I no kill Frank. Someone kill him. You find!"

I pushed the chair back and stood up from the desk. "All right, Mrs Deauville I'm going to let you go, DC Lawson will take you next door to the Incident Room and give you some lunch and get you to make a formal statement. When that's done WPC Green will take you home, OK?"

She nodded sniffily.

"Mr Yavarov you are free to accompany Mrs Deauville and render her assistance, or you are free to go. If you want to stay we'll get you lunch too."

"I will help Mrs Deauville with her statement," he said.

I took Crabbie to one side. "When you let her go, have WPC Green drive her home, but get her to take her time about it. I want the house watched and I want the team to be in place by the time she arrives."

"To what end?"

"If it were me and the police hadn't found my lock-up garage full of drugs I'd want to slip out in the middle of the night and destroy the evidence. Or I might just want to fly the coop."

"It'll mean a call to Special Branch to get a covert team," he said.

"It'll be worth it if we can catch her in the act of destroying the evidence. Charge her with obstruction of justice and use that as leverage against her."

"Leverage for what? I don't think she knows anything about the murder."

"Everybody knows something."

A half dozen phone calls later Crabbie came back with a face even more sour than usual.

"What's the matter?"

"Special Branch won't do it. They say it's not a priority."

"They won't help at all?"

"They say they can't justify the expense of a team for a low-level drug dealer in Carrickfergus."

"Well that's odd. Thought they would have jumped at the chance. All right, no big deal, we'll do it ourselves, then. Find a few keen reservists to watch the place."

"It'll be over-time. Inspector Dalziel—"

"I'll pay for it out of my own pocket if I have to. Mrs Deauville will probably clock them and stay indoors, but at least our evidence won't be destroyed and she won't run for the airport."

"Aye. OK. A couple of reservists to watch the house. Then what?"

"You and I are going to go to Larne to interview this Morrison bloke."

I went to my office to get my portable tape recorder when there was a knock at the door.

The door opened and an ashen Chief Inspector McArthur came in with the early edition of the *Belfast Telegraph*.

"Page two," he said.

I opened up the paper and there over the top half of page two was a picture of yesterday's chaotic crime scene: the broken police tape, the crowd milling around the body, the goddamn goat sniffing at the victim's denim jacket.

"Fuck!" I gasped.

"Read the story, Duffy."

The story was, if anything, worse:

CROSSBOW CHAOS IN CARRICKFERGUS
By Stephen O'Toole

A murder case seemed to confound the officers of Carrickfergus CID yesterday morning. For much of the day this reporter watched as a parade of RUC men bungled an investigation into the death of a man in the Sunnylands area of the town. The victim, a Mr Francis Deauville, lay in his driveway at 15 Mountbatten Terrace for almost three hours while his neighbours milled around the body smoking cigarettes and a goat nibbled at the victim's clothing. No effort was made to "secure the crime scene" nor were forensic officers summoned to the murder.

"Is this the way murders are always handled in Carrickfergus?" I asked one uniformed RUC officer who merely a grunted a response.

The head of Carrickfergus CID, Inspector Sean Duffy, could not be reached for comment. Duffy is a controversial figure at the Carrick RUC barracks. He has been disciplined more than once by the police tribunal and on one occasion was demoted a full rank apparently because of incompetence. This murder case seems certainly to have "made a goat" of Duffy and his fellow officers in Carrickfergus RUC. Local independent Unionist Councillor Leslie Hale told this reporter that he wasn't surprised by the goat incident and that "Carrick RUC had been a joke for years." Neighbours on Mountbatten Terrace were similarly distressed by the serial blunders from the local police. Chairman of the local residents' association the Reverend William McFaul spoke of the "absolute foul language" and "rudeness" of one policeman whose identity this reporter was unable to confirm.

> Forensic officers did not arrive on the scene until nearly
> four hours after the body was . . .

I let the paper fall to the floor.

I felt light, my head was swimming. I put an arm out to steady myself.

"Fucking hell," I groaned.

"What happened yesterday, Sean?"

"What?"

"What happened yesterday, Sean?"

"It's complicated."

"Uncomplicate it."

I took a deep breath. "Well, it was a little crazy at first, sir. The victim's wife stabbed Sergeant McCrabban and Dalziel made him go to the hospital."

"Where were you when this was going on?"

"I was on my holidays, sir. I was in Donegal in the morning. It wasn't even my case!"

"Did you assume command when you arrived?"

"I had to. Because of Kenny Dalziel's blundering only young Lawson was there. He sent everybody away."

"Hmmm."

"How badly am I fucked?"

"I don't know. Chief Superintendent Strong has come down again, doubtless he'll want a word with you."

"Jesus! Strong has seen this?"

"Sean, be under no illusions, by the end of the day the Chief Constable will have seen this."

"Jesus, Mary and Joseph! What can I do?"

"Don't do anything. Have a cup of tea. No booze! Sit tight. I'll see what—"

Another knock at the door.

"Who is it?"

"Duffy, is that you in there?" Strong asked and then came

in without waiting for a reply. I've seen less purple beetroots than Strong's cheeks and forehead. Always a tall man, he looked even taller somehow when he was pissed off. His nose was a furious red and his ginger beard and salt-and-pepper hair were almost standing on end. As an ex-boilermaker who'd apprenticed in the Clydeside yards before transferring to Belfast in the early 60s he had impressively massive hands and shoulders. All this combined with his tight dark green uniform and Chief Superintendent's pips meant that he cut an imposing figure on even his good days.

Strong looked at the Chief Inspector and the spilled newspaper on the floor.

"Make yourself scarce, McArthur, I'll talk to Duffy here," Strong said in that gravelly Govan accent of his.

"Yes, sir," McArthur said.

When he'd gone, Strong went over to the drinks trolley and poured us both a healthy measure of Jura. He handed me a glass and sat down.

"Details, lad. Don't leave anything out even if it looks bad for you and your men. If you lie to me now it'll go much worse for you in the long run."

I told him everything in as cool and dispassionate voice as I could muster. The Jura helped, as Jura always does. But in truth my bap was ringing and I was having trouble keeping it together. Strong listened, drank his whisky and asked a few pointed questions along the way.

When I was done he nodded to himself and stood. "Right. It looks like you did all you could, Duffy. It was just an unlucky set of circumstances, that's all. I'll get the PR boys to formulate a response to the *Bel Tel* and any other media who pick up this story. And I'll talk to the Chief Constable when he calls."

"Is he going to call?"

"He'll have to. The minister will be on him and he'll be looking for blood. But he's not going to get it. I'm not having some jackal in the gutter press taking down one of my men."

A huge wave of relief washed over me. John Strong – son and grandson of Clydebank shop stewards – was a good man to have on your side.

"Thank you, sir."

"You are to talk to nobody, Duffy."

"No, sir."

"If anyone from the press calls you have no comment."

"No comment. Understood, sir."

"Do you have a suspect in this case?"

"No, sir. Looks like the wife didn't do it, so it's a bit of a mystery."

"That's the last thing we need. How so, a mystery?" Strong asked.

"Well, there's the unusual murder weapon and no claim of responsibility from any of the paramilitary factions or that DAADD group that sometimes kills alleged drug dealers."

"You can rule out the wife? I hear she's an immigrant? And she's clearly violent."

"Well, there's no 'definitely' in a case like this, but we were all pretty impressed by her testimony. A second man, also an alleged drug dealer, was shot a few nights ago. He lived. I was just on my way to interview him."

"Second man, eh? Also with a crossbow?"

"Yes, sir."

"Aha! So this is some kind of vigilante out to get drug dealers?"

"Could be, sir. I had young Lawson check to see if there had been any heroin overdoses or deaths in Carrick or Belfast lately."

"How would that tie in?"

"Revenge? Kid overdoses and the parents seek revenge on the dealer. Or on all the dealers. But there have been no over-dose deaths of heroin this year. And Lawson says that the deaths from last year don't link back to Deauville."

"And before that?"

"Deauville wasn't in the heroin trade. He was in England in the bank-robbing trade . . . So I suppose that brings us back to DAADD."

"If one of the paramilitary groups or DAADD was to take responsibility for the murder, would the case go away?"

"It wouldn't be solved, sir, but—"

"But what?"

"We'd probably yellow the file. Case like that almost never gets solved unless there's eyewitness testimony or forensic evidence."

"So I could then tell the Chief Constable that the case was closed?"

"It wouldn't be closed but it would be yellowed – no further action by Carrick CID, pending additional evidence."

Strong nodded to himself. "That would satisfy him. And it would probably satisfy those bastards in the press."

"Yes, sir. About that. They said some very inaccurate things about me. Maybe I should contact a lawyer or—"

"No! No lawyers. No comment. All you will do is work diligently and quietly on getting this case out of your inbox as quickly as possible."

"Yes, sir."

"And no doubt – this being bloody Belfast – there will be some kind of atrocity along in a few days to get the press slavering for someone else's hide."

"Yes, sir."

"I'll deal with the Chief Constable. Don't pick up your phone. In fact get out of the office, now. You say you have more following up to do?"

"Yes, sir, in Larne, sir. Interview the first victim."

"Good. Go!"

"Yes, sir . . . uhm, thank you, sir."

Chief Superintendent Strong stood up and offered me his big hairy boilermaker's paw. "Aye, like I say, I remember your work in the Lily Bigelow case. You did right by her and by Eddie McBain. Ed was my mentor and you did right by him. You're a good policeman, Duffy. A good copper. I don't care what the file says on you."

"Thank you, sir."

"And I am not going to have some scumbag drug dealer and some vermin journalist destroy your career, Duffy."

"I'm very grateful, sir."

"Now get out of here before your phone starts ringing and they draw you deeper into the bloody web."

8: IVAN MORRISON

The sun setting behind the Antrim Hills. Rain pounding the windscreen. Sea spray on the side windows. The Land Rover swaying in the twenty-knot crosswind as we drove along the Acreback Road.

We had no radio reception at all and Crabbie wasn't talking. He could go a thousand years and not mention the embarrassing story in the *Belfast Telegraph*. If someone was going to bring it up it would have to be me and I didn't feel like it.

"I was down here earlier this morning," I said as we drove through Magheramorne.

"Oh aye?"

"Beth had me down looking at a house."

"Where?"

"The Ballypollard road."

"Oh I know that road very well. You'd only be ten minutes from me. Well, ten minutes the way you drive. Lovely wee road, that. Have you got a view?"

"I'm not sure I want to move down here."

"It's a lovely wee quiet spot."

"I like Coronation Road."

"But Beth doesn't?"

"She says no one talks to her."

"Stop me if I'm being too personal but she's a Protestant, isn't she?"

"Oh yeah, Prod as the day is long. It's not that. It's a class thing, not a religious thing. They're working-class Prods, she's some kind of posh Prod from Larne."

"So you don't want to move?"

"Not really. But the house is going to take two years to build anyway. Lot could happen in two years."

"That it could," Crabbie said reflectively. "But it is very nice around here."

"Beth and I had a row about it. I overreacted."

"Not like you, Sean."

I laughed. "Oh you think you're funny, do you?"

He cleared his throat. "There's a wee place down this way I'm thinking of buying."

"Oh yeah? An extra field or two?"

"Considerably more than that. In fact, I'm thinking of throwing my hand in, if that's the correct expression."

"What do you mean?"

"Well, old Kerry McBride is looking to sell her acres now she's turned seventy, and she'd give them to me for a good price. That's all cattle land of course."

"Of course."

"It would put me up to 150 head and even if I got rid of the sheep, which I would, that's still a full-time job, isn't it?"

I looked at him. "What are you talking about, Crabbie?"

"I'm more of a hobby farmer at the moment. Helen does most of it, but if I take this plot, well, I'll have to come in full time, won't I?"

"You're quitting?"

"Thinking about it. Thinking seriously about it."

"You'll leave me and Lawson in the lurch?"

"Carrickfergus is more of a two-man station anyway."

"What are you talking about? We've got a murder on our hands."

"Our first murder in nearly a year."

"The Troubles could spiral up at any moment. You know they could. These things come in waves."

"Sean . . . I know. But with the farm. I have a young family," he said guiltily.

"Crabbie, mate, you can't leave because of one bad day. One bad shellacking in the press."

"Oh it's not that. I don't care about that. I've been thinking about this for some time. I've been neither one thing nor the other for a few years now. A man cannot serve two masters. A house fernenst itself cannot stand. I cannot do the farm and be a Detective Sergeant in the RUC."

Not this on top of everything else. Crabbie couldn't go. I needed him. Was that panic I was feeling?

Fear?

It was a dangerous job, a dangerous job for a man with a young daughter and you needed a steady hand by your side. Crabbie had always been that steady hand. Crabbie would always be the guy going down into the engine room to fix the warp drive and save the ship. I liked Lawson, Lawson was good, but he wasn't the Crabman.

Jesus, having trouble breathing again.

Deep breaths. Deep breaths.

"You can't go. You can't go and let Kenny Dalziel run the station. You just can't."

"The man's a fool," Crabbie agreed.

"And a scoundrel. McArthur as much as told me he beats his wife."

"The blackguard. Who hits a woman? To think we have to share a breakroom with such a fellow."

"Indeed and if he's the gaffer we can't take him outside and give him a hiding. I like that word blackguard by the way. It doesn't get enough of an airing these days. Listen, mate, if you go and Dalziel is the chief, what then? I might as well bloody quit too."

"What would you do?"

"I don't know. Beth's da's loaded. Maybe he'd give me a job."

If Beth and I are still a couple?

Crabbie nodded. "If you go and I go I suppose they'd make Lawson a detective sergeant and bring in a young DC . . . but I don't think you should resign, Sean. You are one of the best detectives I have ever worked with."

"So are you. Please don't go, mate. We need you. I need you," I said.

"I'm still thinking about it," Crabbie said.

I leaned against the steering wheel.

"Everything's just spinning out of control today," I muttered.

"Eyes on the road, Sean, come on. I'll put the radio on for you. You like Radio 3, don't you? Let me see if the reception's better."

I pulled over. "You drive." We swapped seats and as luck would have it, Arvo Pärt's *Tabula Rasa* was playing, which worked perfectly with the rain's assault on the bulletproof windscreen.

We drove to the Moyle Hospital in a contemplative silence.

A man in a raincoat who looked like a reporter but who could have just been a man in a raincoat was standing outside.

"Fifty quid if you run that journalist-looking fucker over," I said.

Crabbie ignored me and parked the Rover but it was a wasted trip, for Ivan Morrison had checked himself out three hours earlier.

While Crabbie got Morrison's home address from the matron I took the opportunity to get my asthma prescriptions filled at the on-site chemist. A pharmacist showed me how to work the inhalers. It wasn't that complicated.

Crabbie came back with the address.

"18 Old Wyncairn Road," he said.

"You know where that is?"

"No idea, but there's a map in the Rover."

Outside into the rain. Arvo Pärt. Ten minutes getting lost. Another ten finding the house. Another ten and we would have missed Ivan completely as he was nearly finished packing. The house was a cheaply built post-war prefab that smelled of damp, desperation and dope. It was built in a row behind a slaughter house at the bottom of a hill.

We parked the Rover and got out. Someone was playing Jackson C. Frank's eponymous first – and only – album which seemed apropos for the day, the estate, the weather and, you know, just life in general.

The slaughter house was quiet but it gave up the terrible stench of fear and sawdust and blood and murder.

"It reeks here," I said.

"Aye, it's bad," Crabbie agreed and he had a farm.

We knocked on the living-room window and I showed my warrant card.

"Carrick RUC," I said.

"I told youse everything," a man said from inside the house.

"You can tell us again."

He reluctantly opened the front door and we went inside.

Clothes all over the floor. A duffel bag and a suitcase open and being loaded up.

I looked at him. Looked at his twenty-two-year-old-going-on-fifty face. With his short hair and his pink skin and his beady black eyes he was like a lab rat who'd been undergoing a terrible series of experiments to see exactly when he would have a mental breakdown.

"This better be quick. I've a ferry to catch," he said.

"We want to know who shot you," Crabbie said.

"I didn't see him."

"How do you know it was a he?"

"Didn't see her either."

"One man or two?"

"I told all this to Larne RUC."

"So you won't mind telling us as well."

"I've no idea who shot me. It was dark, I was walking along, fucking huge fucking pain in my back and I went down like a ton of bricks. Car driving off pronto."

"What type of car?"

"I don't know."

"Have you had any threats lately?"

"Threats about what?"

"We know you're a drug dealer."

"Who told you that?"

"Look, Ivan, we want to help. You are not under arrest, nothing you say will incriminate you. I'm not drugs squad and I give you my word I won't pass any information on to the drugs squad."

"How can I trust you? Never heard of you. Don't know you from Adam. You're not even a Larne peeler. You could be anybody."

I showed him my warrant card again. "Read that. Carrickfergus CID. Not drugs squad, not Special Branch. I'm investigating a murder in Carrick yesterday – you might have heard of it."

"I have heard of it. Why do you think I'm packing?"

"All we want to know is who threatened you."

"I'm not talking. I'm not saying fucking anything to you, pal."

I grabbed the little lab rat by his Fred Perry Polo shirt and flung him into the aluminium walls of his house, aluminium that if it had somehow become sentient would no doubt have relished the action, having been in a previous incarnation the panels of a fighter plane or a Lancaster bomber. Ivan bounced off the briefly happy wall and gave me a hurt look.

"Hey," he said. "You can't do that!"

"You know what I'll have to do next? I'll have to arrest you and hold you as a material witness and maybe I'll throw in a charge of trafficking. I'll personally turn up for your bail hearing and I'll oppose bail and you, my son, will be inside, where anybody can get you for the next six months."

"Why would you do all that?" Ivan asked, still giving me that I-thought-we-were-friends look.

"Cos you're not cooperating."

"What is it you fucking want to know anyway?"

"I want to know who shot you."

"I didn't see who did it and by that I mean I really didn't bloody see who did it. I was walking home from the leisure centre and they just plugged me in the fucking back. That's it. End of story. Now if you don't mind I have to get back to my packing."

"Whither goest thou?"

"Getting the night ferry to Stranraer."

"Has someone told you to leave the country?"

"No. I think the message was clear enough."

"Where are you moving to?"

"Anywhere but here."

"Lucky you."

"Lucky me."

I gave him my card. "Well, if your memory suddenly clears up please don't hesitate to call. You can reverse the charges if you're over in England."

He examined the card and leaned in close to me. "I paid off every week like a choirboy. Thirty per cent of my gross. Not my net. My gross. There was no sense in killing me. Killing me was killing the goose."

"What are you saying?"

"The paramilitaries didn't shoot me. This is something else."

"Like what?"

"I don't know, but I'm not sticking around to find out."

"Come on then, we'll give you a lift to the ferry terminal."

We drove him down to the docks and saw him into the ferry terminal.

Instead of heading back to Carrick I found myself driving out along the Old Glenarm Road and then along the Coast Road.

The rain was still pouring down hard and a light mist was coming in from the sea. Crabbie thought that I'd gotten us lost again.

"Carrick's back that way, I think, Sean," Crabbie said diplomatically.

I stopped the Rover in front of a large, rectangular modern house right on the seashore. It had its own pier and mooring dock and a couple of boats were tied up there. It had big windows facing north and east and although it was all right angles its stylish minimalism worked well with the sea and sky. It was easily three times the size of my parents' cottage in Donegal. And down in the basement there was a twenty-metre three-lane swimming pool.

"Why have we stopped?" Crabbie asked and when I didn't respond he reluctantly spoke to fill the silence. "So who lives here, Sean? It's not Dalziel's house is it? I know he comes from money."

"It's Beth's father's house. She's taken Emma to stay with them for a couple of days."

"Oh."

"Do you think I should do a wee surprise visit?"

"No."

"Why not?"

"You had a row?"

"Aye."

"She's with her mother and father. She wants her space, doesn't she? Away from you."

"Is that what Helen would do?"

"Helen and her father don't get on."

"How come?"

"His new wife, May, hit Thomas for bringing mud in on the kitchen floor."

"Wee Tommy? My godson? The cheek of her. Helen and May had words, then?"

"Helen said that if May ever raised a hand to any of her children again she would put her in the hospital."

I nodded. "She would, too."

"Aye, she would," Crabbie agreed. "A remarkable woman."

I looked at the house for a couple of minutes. A light came on in an upstairs window and there was a brief glimpse of what might have been Beth's silhouette before the light went off again.

I turned the key in the ignition.

"Come on, let's get out of here, I'll drive you home."

Crabbie's house.

Quick hello to Helen and the boys.

Back along the Coast Road and the Old Glenarm Road. Back past Magheramorne and Whitehead and Eden and all the way back to the station

Night shift.

Skeleton crew.

"Have you seen this, Duffy???????????" said a post-it note pinned to a copy of the *Belfast Telegraph* that had been placed on my desk. I binned the paper and examined the note: of course it was Dalziel's handwriting.

I walked down to his office, but he wasn't in.

I took a piece of A4 paper and penned a reply.

"In answer to your note, yes I have seen it, Kenny. Nice work with the question marks by the way, most people would only do three or four, leaving me baffled as to their intent," I wrote.

I left it in the middle of his desk, checked for witnesses, fought the urge to piss in his Yucca plant, and left.

I was about to head home when I saw Yavarov, the Bulgarian translator.

"What are you still doing here? Didn't we let Mrs Deauville go home hours ago?"

"You did. There is a bomb scare on the train lines. No trains to Belfast or Dublin, tonight."

"Do you want me to drive you to a hotel?"

Yavarov smiled ruefully. "Because of the bomb scare and the train cancellations, all the hotels in Belfast are full up."

This didn't surprise me. Belfast only had three hotels in the entire city because they kept getting blown up by the IRA. The Europa Hotel had been destroyed and rebuilt four times since the Troubles had begun.

"There's actually a hotel in Carrick, the Coast Road, they owe me a favour. One of their guests was murdered and I found out who did it," I said. "I'll call them."

"Thank you."

I called up the Coast Road but it was no dice there either, even for Inspector Sean Duffy of Carrick RUC.

"Sorry, they're booked out too," I said.

"How long do these bomb alerts last?"

"They'll usually have the line checked and inspected by the morning."

"I am used to roughing it, maybe I could sleep in one your cells until then?"

"The cells? Nonsense. They're freezing. Come home with me. I've got a spare bedroom at the back."

"Really? It's no trouble?"

"No trouble at all. We'll have to walk though. I didn't take the car into work this morning. It's only a ten-minute hoof-it."

Yavarov agreed, I got my coat and we walked to Coronation Road.

The rain had driven everyone inside so it was a quiet night in the estate.

"This reminds me of parts of Sofia," Yavarov said.

"I'm not sure if that's a compliment or not."

"Sofia was not as heavily bombed as some cities in the war," Yavarov said, which didn't really clarify matters.

When we got to #113, I heated up the remains of a previous night's chilli con carne and went upstairs to turn on the paraffin heater.

"You have a daughter?" Yavarov asked, looking at the doll collection and Disney Princess colouring books and assuming that they weren't mine.

"Wife and daughter are down staying with her parents for a few days."

Yavarov raised an eyebrow but said nothing.

"You want a drink?"

"You have vodka?" he asked.

"Do I have vodka? Of course. I make a mean vodka martini and an even meaner vodka gimlet."

Yavarov grimaced. "Just vodka will be sufficient."

I handed him a half full bottle of Absolut blue label and a couple of glasses while I finished the chilli.

"Swedish? I have never had Swedish vodka before," Yavarov said.

"I'm no vodka expert, but I think it's pretty good."

Yavarov poured us a couple of healthy measures.

"*Nazdrave!*" he said and finished his shot. He reflected for a moment before nodding. "You're right, it's good. But there is something, what is the word . . . unwholesome about it."

"Unwholesome? I don't think that can be the word you're after."

"Unwholesome, no that is the word. It tastes of Sweden. It is neutral, clean, antiseptic, healthy."

I nodded.

"I think I know what you need, mate."

I went out to the shed in the rain and came back with a jar of poteen.

I poured him a shot of it.

"What is this?"

"Moonshine. You know what that is?"

He nodded. "You make it?"

"No, a bloke up the road who has a pet lion."

"You are joking with me."

"I wish."

He swallowed down a healthy measure. "This is more like it," he said.

Six more shots and a bottle of wine with the chilli and we would have praised the virtues of paint thinner.

We talked about Bulgaria and Ireland and the lack of any connection at all we could think of between the two countries. I told him that Kenny Dalziel had forbidden me to fly to Bulgaria so the murder of Mr Deauville better not have a complicated international dimension.

"You think such a thing is possible?" Yavarov asked.

"Anything's possible but I think we're probably looking at some kind of internal drug war here, or possibly a vigilante. Most likely it was some lone wolf nutjob among the Proddy paramilitaries. They're not known for attracting a high calibre of personnel."

"You don't think Mrs Deauville did it, then?"

"No. Unless she's a good actress or a KGB agent. She's not a KGB agent?"

"You think the KGB would employ someone like that to work for them?"

"Of course. Last person MI5 would suspect."

"MI5 suspect everyone," Yavarov said sadly.

"You're not KGB, are you?"

"In Bulgaria there is no KGB."

"What's the Bulgarian equivalent?"

"One does not speak of such things," he said.

"You are one, aren't you? I can tell. I've met quite a few spooks in my time. Don't worry, it doesn't bother me. KGB, CIA, MI5, you're all the same. Who gives a shit?"

"In Bulgaria it is called the Durzhavna Sigurnost. The State Security Police. But I am not Durzhavna. Believe me, if I was I would not have had to take the train up here today."

"Tell me off the record about Mrs Deauville. What's her

story? What do the files tell you?" I asked, now that he was in confidence-spilling mood.

"There is nothing to tell. She was a travel agent. She met Deauville and apparently they fell in love."

"How did she get to leave Bulgaria?"

"Her husband paid off the right people."

"Wouldn't that cost a lot of money?"

"Not much these days. Ten years ago it was almost impossible to get an exit visa. In 1988 it is a different story."

We finished the bottle of Absolut and I played Yavarov my copy of *Tabula Rasa*.

A strange look flitted across Yavarov's face. "Are you homosexual, Duffy?" he asked.

A momentary hesitation before I answered: "No."

The strange look vanished. "I like this music, but it is so sad."

"You're lucky I didn't put on the Shostakovich."

It was after one, so I showed Yavarov to his bedroom at the back of the house. The room with the weirdly unobstructed view all the way to the massive cranes of Harland and Wolff shipyard eight miles distant across the lough.

"I'll leave you to it then, Pytor. Bathroom just down the hall."

He offered me his hand and I shook it. "You're a good man, Duffy. A good man. I would help you if I could. But I cannot," he said.

"What do you mean?"

"My duty is to protect a Bulgarian citizen. Her interests must come first."

"Did she tell you something about her husband's murder?"

Yavarov shook his head.

"What did she tell you? Did she see who did it? Did she do it?"

"She did not do it and she did not see who killed him," Yavarov said emphatically.

"Then what?"

"Nothing . . . I am drunk."

"You're as drunk as me. What did she tell you?"

"She told me nothing. She does not know anything. She did not see anything. I am just talking. I am drunk. I am not a good Bulgarian. I get drunk very easily."

He yawned and swayed there for a moment until he found a convenient wall. He picked up the cat and put it down again when it gave him a dirty look.

"I will tell you Bulgarian joke," he said.

"No jokes, tell me what she told you."

"A squirrel is in a pine tree, when all of a sudden, it starts shaking. He looks down, and sees an elephant climbing the tree. 'What are you doing? Why are you climbing my tree?' the squirrel calls down to the elephant. 'I'm coming up there to eat some pears!' the elephant responds. 'You fool! This is a pine tree! There aren't any pears up here!' The elephant looks perplexed for a moment, and then says, 'Well, I brought my own pears.'"

Yavarov burst into laughter and I smiled at him. I put my hand on his shoulder. "You'd tell me if you knew anything, wouldn't you, Pytor? We're old pals now," I said.

"Old pals," he agreed. "Inspector Duffy of Belfast who has Swedish vodka and listens to Estonian classical music. And Pytor Yavarov, the son of Alexander Yavarov who was for a time in 1943 an attaché to King Boris III."

"King Boris, eh?"

"Much maligned man, Tsar Boris. History does not forgive but I say this: only two countries under Nazi occupation in all of Europe save every one of their Jewish citizens: Denmark and Bulgaria. Yes?"

"OK, mate, I believe you. King Boris – good egg. I gotta go to bed. The bathroom's down the hall, there's some spare pyjamas in the linen cupboard, don't fuck with the paraffin heater – that thing's dangerous."

I left him to it and went to my room. I was too exhausted to write the conversation down and indeed I forgot all about it until a few weeks later. It had been a bloody awful day on the whole. And my head would be a bear in the morning.

9: DAADD KNOWS BEST

Downstairs to get the milk before the starlings got to work on it. Too late: the gold top sipped from, the silver top stabbed.

Frost on the ground. Blue sky above the Antrim Hills. Mooing of cows, baaing of sheep, growling of diggers as Greater Belfast pushed deeper into the Irish countryside . . .

I took a deep breath. In a couple of years Coronation Road wouldn't be special any more. When I'd first moved here it was the last street in Carrick before the wild country of County Antrim began – country of the Ulaidh and Finn and Sweeney among the nightingales . . . But with all the construction going on now, by 1990 Coronation Road would just be part of the Greater Belfast sprawl.

Moving wouldn't be so bad. Beth was probably right.

The cat strolled up the garden path and meowed at my feet. I showed him the vandalised milk bottle.

"See this? What do you do to earn your keep around here? Keeping the starlings away from the bloody milk is your—"

A silver Jaguar was driving up Coronation Road. I put down the cat. A tall pinched man in a corduroy jacket and flat cap was driving the Jag, slowly looking for parking as if he owned the place. Who knows? Maybe he did. Maybe he'd built this street and named it back in 1953.

I clocked the number plate to confirm my worst fears: "JAG-7" it said.

"Shite," I muttered, closed the door and brought the milk in.

Yavarov was in the kitchen eating toast and drinking coffee and wearing my old red pyjamas.

"Morning," I said.

"Morning. I made coffee, have some," he said.

"Thanks."

"This was excellent drink we had last night. I can't remember it but it must have been good if you wake up without a hangover. Only bad vodka gives you a . . ." I tuned him out and lit a Marlboro. I don't care what Dr Havercamp or anybody says: a Marlboro and a good black coffee fights the demons like nothing else.

"I made toast, would you like some?" Yavarov asked.

"How did you get the toaster to work? That thing baffles me."

"It was easy."

There was a knock at the front door. I swallowed the coffee and took another pull of the ciggie.

Another knock.

"There is someone at your door."

"I know."

A third knock.

"Do you want me to answer it?"

"I'll do it."

I walked down the hall and opened the front door.

"Hello, Hector," I said.

"Hello, Sean."

"What can I do for you?"

"Elizabeth needs her books."

"What books?"

"For her studies."

"Why didn't she come and get them?"

"She asked me to do it."

Beth's father and I glared at one another. If he'd stood up straight he would have been half a foot taller than me, about six five or so, but he was in his mid sixties now and his whole body was crooked. His hair was grey and he was wearing thick George Smiley glasses. He looked, in fact, like a stretched Alec Guinness, but without Guinness's gravitas or heft. He wasn't a frail man – he kept himself fit through golfing and sailing – but there was something insubstantial about him. Some void at the heart of him that reminded me of all these upper-middle-class Prods who grew up in the mid-century good times of Northern Ireland, when working-class Prods and *every* Catholic knew their place.

"What's going on, Hector?"

"Will you let me in to get her stuff?"

"What's going on? I thought she was only staying there for a couple of days?"

His grey eyes narrowed. "What did you do to her?" he growled.

"What are you talking about?"

"If you laid a finger on her, so help me, I don't care if you are a policeman, you're a fucking dead man."

I was taken aback for two reasons: it was a good few months since I'd had a death threat, but more impressively, I'd never heard Hector swear before. And swearing in defence of one's daughter was a good thing.

"Are you going to let me in or not? I need to get some things for the baby, too."

"Help yourself," I said standing aside. "The baby's room is next to ours upstairs, Beth's office with her books is in the spare bedroom at the back."

Hector tramped upstairs.

"Is anything wrong?" Yavarov asked.

"Just a sec," I said and held up a finger while I dialled Larne. Someone picked up on the third ring.

"Hello?"

"Beth is that you?"

"Yes."

"What the hell's going on now? I thought we just had a fucking tiff?" was my less than diplomatic opening.

"Sean, I just sent my dad to get some of my things, you're not rowing with him, are you?"

"I thought you said you were coming back today."

"I never said that."

"We just had a row. It was no big deal. And you were right. It's a great house. It's a lovely gesture. I said I was sorry."

"Sean, please, don't argue with my father. He's not a young man."

"I'm not arguing with him. He's upstairs getting things for Emma and your books! Why?"

She sighed. "I told you. I think we need a little time apart to think things over."

"You never said anything of the sort. What things? Things were going OK. I'd smoothed it all over with my natural charm and I already said sorry about the house."

"Sean, please, can I call you in a couple of days?"

"No. Let me drive down there with your father—"

"No! Please, Sean, I know that you're a reasonable man. Just give me a couple of days to get my bearings. I'll give you a call. I had a talk with Mum and Dad last night and it got me thinking—"

"Your bloody father, wasn't it?"

"No, well . . . look, I just want a few days. What's wrong with that?"

"I miss Emma. And I know she misses me."

"I know."

"So?"

"I'll call you."

"When?"

"What day is today?"

"Saturday."

"I'll call you tomorrow."

A long pause while Yavarov pottered about in the kitchen, the cat meowed and Hector made a hell of a racket upstairs.

"OK, Beth. Call me tomorrow. I'm not working. I'll be home."

"Fine."

"Kiss Emma for me."

"I will."

"I love you."

" . . . bye, Sean," she said and then in a whisper she added, "love you" and quickly hung up. I put the phone in the crook.

It wasn't a very original thought but I articulated it anyway: women – who could understand them?

She loved me. That was only the second or third time she'd actually said that.

I walked into the kitchen, confused, emotional.

Yavarov refilled my coffee cup.

"May I ask what's happening, or would that be rude?"

"Girlfriend's father is upstairs getting some of her stuff."

"She left you?"

"It's more complicated than that."

"Did you beat her? Is she afraid of you?"

"I never laid a finger on her and don't say 'that's where you went wrong' or anything glib and Eastern European like that."

Before Yavarov could say anything Hector came down the stairs with the cot filled with books. The cot was enormous and made of cedar, so Hector must have been stronger than he looked.

"Let me help you with that," I said, taking one end of the cot.

"I too will help!" Yavarov said.

Hector saw Yavarov and me in our matching pyjamas and gave us a withering look.

A lesser man might have felt the need to explain Yavarov's

presence and started babbling about missed trains and bomb scares but I didn't feel the need to explain anything to Hector Macdonald.

I took one end of the cot and we walked out to the Jaguar. The boot was only big enough for a set of golf clubs so we put everything in the back seat instead.

I closed the back door and looked at Hector.

"Emma needs to be burped twice after the midnight feed," I said. "Beth's not usually up for that one."

"I'll tell Jane," he said curtly.

"Oh, and you should remind her to study for her tutorial on Monday. It's Dr Byrne and he's a taskmaster."

Hector sniffed. "I don't know about that. We've been talking about having her switch to business administration. Literature's a bit useless isn't it? In life, I mean."

Beth had two older brothers but one was a site manager in Chicago and the other was running a mine in South Africa. Neither could be relied upon to take over Macdonald Construction when the old man finally called it quits. Was Beth being groomed now? Was that the plan?

"That's right, books are rubbish, aren't they?" was all I said, trying to keep the sarcasm level down to a 3 or 4.

"Some good reading in the paper though these days isn't there? I read about your latest case. Page two of the *Belfast Telegraph*."

I opened the car door. "Safe home, Hector."

He nodded, got into the Jag, closed the door and drove away.

"I do not like this man, you are lucky to escape from such a family connection," Yavarov said.

"Hmmm. Come on, get dressed and I'll drive you to the train station."

I finished the coffee, dressed, took a hit on my asthma inhaler, packed the emergency inhaler, looked under the Beemer for bombs and drove Yavarov to Carrick train station. I saw him to the ticket booth where he got a through ticket to Dublin. We shook hands and I gave him my card. I went across the road to the Railway Tavern which opened at 10 o'clock on Saturday mornings for the football crowd.

I ordered a pint of Guinness and a double whisky chaser. I thought about Dr Havercamp. How many fucking units is this, you bastard?

I gave the barman a fiver and asked if he had any crisps. Crisps and Guinness for breakfast: it was like my single days.

The Railway Tavern was a hardcore UVF bar that didn't look kindly on strangers but I was wearing my black drainpipes, my DM boots and a blood-stained Undertones T-shirt under my black leather jacket. To complete the picture of a possibly unhinged psycho I hadn't shaved and I had a *I-would-fucking-love-you-to-say-something* look in my eyes.

I finished the Guinness, looked under the Beemer for bombs and drove to the station.

The angry walk up the stairs to the Incident Room left me breathless and I took a discreet pull on the emergency inhaler. It worked like a miracle and my breathing calmed down immediately. I automatically reached for a cigarette, but realising the paradox instead crunched the packet and threw it in the bin just outside the Incident Room door.

Crabbie heard the bin rattle and opened the door. He was smiling, which made me immediately suspicious.

"It's not the End of Days, is it? Jesus is back and he's declared the Presbyterians as the only true believers?"

"What?"

"Nothing. You look pleased. What's going on?"

"A break in the case. DAADD haven't claimed responsibility for the killing but intel spotted this story in *Republican News* and faxed it to us: